ROGUE RETRIBUTION

ROGUE RETRIBUTION

ROGUE AGENTS OF MAGIC™ BOOK 4

TR CAMERON   MICHAEL ANDERLE   MARTHA CARR

DISRUPTIVE IMAGINATION

LMBPN Publishing
PMB 196, 2540 South Maryland Pkwy
Las Vegas, NV 89109

Version 1.00, December, 2021
ebook ISBN: 978-1-68500-616-7
Print ISBN: 978-1-68500-617-4

THE ROGUE RETRIBUTION TEAM

Thanks to our JIT Readers:

Dorothy Lloyd
Dave Hicks
Wendy L Bonell
Diane L. Smith
Zacc Pelter

If we've missed anyone, please let us know!

Editor
Skyhunter Editing Team

DEDICATION

For those who seek wonder around every corner and in each turning page. And, as always, for Dylan and Laurel.

— *TR Cameron*

CHAPTER ONE

D iana pressed her foot down on the accelerator, urging the rental Dodge Charger to increased effort as the speedometer kicked up over eighty miles per hour. The engine growled, and she smiled at the sound. It was one of the few non-electric vehicles available to rent, and she'd willingly paid a premium to drive it. Or, more accurately, the cracked government credit card she was using had paid a premium for it. *That's not the only thing the government's going to be on the hook for today.*

The interior was all soft black leather and hard plastic in the same shade. The car was perfect, except for the absent stick shift. Unfortunately, vehicles with autonomous modes tended not to have manual transmissions for obvious reasons. An evergreen air freshener hung from the mirror, filling the car with its forest scent. She let out a quiet curse as she swung around a slow-moving vehicle, one that suggested the driver's parentage might've been somewhat problematic.

Kayleigh's voice came over the comm set in her ear.

"Everything looks good. The convoy is nearing the interception point on schedule. Nearby traffic is all as anticipated." The tech watched over the operation through the mobile eyes of a drone flying high above their targets to avoid detection.

Hank's deep tones answered, "Foolish people. Should've had more guards on something this valuable." The team's most physically imposing member was currently behind the wheel of another vehicle trailing the military conveyances.

Cara, her second-in-command, was difficult to hear through the *hiss* of the wind whipping by as she rode in the back of the pickup truck. "I wouldn't get too cocky. For all we know, this is some sort of elaborate trap. It would be a perfect example of our luck lately if it was."

Their infomancer, Deacon, replied, "We have flawless security on this. I'll eat my hat if they know we're coming."

Rath the troll, whose voice was also thready thanks to the wind whipping by, answered, "You don't wear a hat."

Kayleigh quipped, "I'll buy him one. Something large and indigestible."

"It would have to be large to fit that head," Rath replied.

Deacon sighed. "Cruel. True, but still cruel."

Diana interrupted the banter. "I make it thirty seconds to intercept."

"Confirmed," Rath agreed.

"Anyone have a reason to abort?" No answers were forthcoming, and she gave a sharp nod of satisfaction. "Excellent. Rambo, the first move is all yours."

Rath banked to continue following the golden path displayed atop the darkened landscape in his goggles. The wings attached to the harness wrapped around his body kept him aloft quite effectively, as long as he concentrated on avoiding the downdrafts. He wore his normal tactical outfit, which included the flying gear, an equipment belt, and a bulletproof vest full of throwing knives, as well as sheaths on his belt that held his combat batons.

Today, he had a little something extra. He pulled the EMP grenade from his belt, pressed the button to prime it, and flicked the switch over to activate its magnetic mode. "Gwen, plot an attack path to the lead vehicle."

The female voice of his suit's AI replied, "Yes." He'd been flying parallel to the convoy, sufficiently far away that hopefully he wouldn't be noticed but still close enough to act quickly. They'd gone into the operation with a plan to eliminate any aerial support that might be present, but no drones other than theirs were tracking the trucks. *Hank's right. Foolish.* A Humvee led the convoy, and another held position at the back, each containing the heat signatures of four occupants.

The three tractor-trailers that occupied the space between the smaller vehicles showed no such signals, which meant someone was either remotely or autonomously controlling them and thus ripe for the picking. Deacon's research had revealed a good haul of equipment would be inside. The military was shipping gear from one location to another in preparation for a frequent government move to close an older base and open a newer facility. Cara had suggested the purpose for the move was that the government simply liked to spend money, and Rath saw no reason to disagree.

In any case, it offered them an opportunity, and it was up to him to start the show. The artificial intelligence contained within his equipment projected an orange line in his goggles. It ended in a box indicating where he should drop the EMP. He curved onto that path, angling slightly downward to gain speed. When he reached the center of the box, he dropped the EMP and called, "Fifteen seconds."

Diana replied, "Acknowledged. Rendezvous with Khan."

He frowned at the command, having argued before the operation that he should be part of any fight that might come. His entreaties hadn't convinced his life partner and leader to let him do so. With a sigh, he replied, "Okay," and angled off to the side, where another member of their team waited in a backup vehicle as insurance in case something went wrong.

Cara gripped the lip of the open window between the pickup truck's cab, where Hank sat behind the wheel, and the bed where she currently crouched as if her life depended on it. She frowned at the wind's continuing attack on her short hair, which caused it to whip around obnoxiously. The surrounding darkness made it possible to forget how fast they were going until Hank gunned the engine and tried to throw her off.

She squeezed harder with one hand, grabbed the EMP disc from her belt, and primed it with the other. She threw the object when the pickup was at the Humvee's six o'clock, and it flew forward and snapped magnetically onto the back. Then Hank pulled ahead, and she waved at the soldiers inside the vehicle as they passed. Her device was timed with Rath's, connected wirelessly through their comm system to ensure that they would detonate simultaneously. They did.

The trailing Humvee immediately fell back as the grenade killed all the electronics inside it. A window in her glasses displayed the take from the drone flying above the scene, where the lead Humvee suddenly pulled off the road, also clearly disabled. The convoy and her truck flashed by it, and she gave a satisfied nod at the confirmation that it hadn't crashed, only fallen away from the chase. *Don't want to seriously hurt Army folks just doing their jobs if we can help it.*

"Hercules, get me close. It's time to see what's inside our presents."

Diana pressed the accelerator to the floor, surged past the third truck in line, and moved to do the same to the middle one, bound for the vehicle that was now leading the convoy. "Got it, Deke?"

The infomancer replied, "I have the wheel."

She pressed the button to lower the window and climbed out, making her way up to the roof. She summoned a thin barrier of force magic to assist, blocking the wind so she could more easily and safely reach the top. When the Charger pulled up alongside her target, she instinctively calculated the angles and blasted a burst of force magic against the car's roof, sending her flying in an arc toward the top of the eighteen-wheeler.

She landed a third of the way forward from the rear doors and drew the line of incendiary cord that Khan had prepared for each of them from her belt. She quickly made a circle large enough to jump through, then set it off. It burned through the roof, and the metal disc fell in and hit with a *clang*.

Diana leapt in after it, excited to see what goodies might lie within. When she passed through the vehicle's skin, her display came alive with heat signals, showing several figures waiting inside the truck.

She growled, "Bastards were smart enough to bring guards along. Engaging."

CHAPTER TWO

Diana's warning came as Cara was making her leap from the pickup's bed onto the top of the tractor-trailer. She landed cleanly, squinting into the wind. Her display indicated that the truck underneath her was at eighty-one miles per hour on the long, flat interstate. A cylindrical force barrier wrapped around her for protection as she laid out the incendiary cord on the trailer's roof. It went off, and she tossed in a pair of grenades, one flash-bang, and one stun. She stepped into the hole a moment later.

The space inside was rendered in sharp detail with a green tint as the lowlight function of her glasses kicked in. Instead of being logically loaded in a cluster at one end of the trailer, pallets supporting tall stacks of crates were positioned haphazardly in the large rectangle. If she hadn't already known the Army had prepared for an assault on the convoy, that arrangement would've confirmed it.

Either they noticed Deacon's hack, or they're being smart.

Probably the latter. Her Army background gave her respect for the military that some of her colleagues didn't feel.

The arrangement of the pallets created a highly defensible maze she would have to pass through to eliminate the opposition. *Well, I'd have to pass through it if I was less well-equipped or less talented, anyway.* Cara grabbed another pair of discs from her belt, tossed them around the corners nearest her, and charged toward the rear of the truck. Fewer enemies lay in that direction, and she couldn't afford to leave them at her back.

Hank's voice came over the comm. "Are we aborting?"

Cara and Diana replied simultaneously. "Hell no." She laughed as the boss continued, "If we can't handle these chuckleheads, we should give up and turn ourselves in."

Hank replied, "Affirmative, heading for the middle one."

Cara's careful advance kept her safe as the display in her glasses shifted to heat mode. They revealed two figures between her and the back of the truck, one on either side of the manufactured aisle. With a small shrug of apology for the damage the move would likely cause them, she shoved her pistol into its holster, lifted both hands, and sent a wave of force magic at the nearest pallets. They slid toward the back of the truck and slammed into the two figures, pinning them between the rear doors and the heavy goods.

She rushed at them, drawing her pistol in her right hand and Demon in her left. The dagger sent a surge of pleasure through her in appreciation for being brought into the fight, which made her chuckle. It was an apt name for the sentient being inside, always mischievous and sometimes vicious. It was always strange holding him without his twin, Angel.

Cara had considered switching their positions, so she drew Angel more often, but everything in the history of magic suggested the right side was angelic and the left demonic. She was superstitious enough not to want to challenge that precedent. *Probably for no reason other than priests back in the day were right-handed, but whatever.*

She found the two figures pinned and used telekinesis to tear their weapons away from them and yank off their helmets. They struggled but were unable to move, much less resist her. A tap on the temple from her shock gloves put them at least temporarily out of the fight.

She spun at a *clatter* from behind, the sound of a fragmentation grenade landing a few feet away. She reflexively threw a shield over the canister to contain the detonation and cringed away. Her last thought before it blew was, *I hope this isn't one of those anti-magic shrapnel grenades Sloan was trying to sell the senator on.*

Hank had chosen this pickup truck for a very specific reason, the winch on the vehicle's front. He smoothly swung the pickup into the gap between the second and third trailers, then hit the button to activate the air compressor sitting on the passenger seat next to him. He'd rigged a magnetic grapnel to the car, and it shot forward out of a launcher similar to the one Rath wore on his arm, but rather bigger, mounted on the hood.

The projectile latched onto the trailer's rear doors, right

at the seam where the two met. A flick of a switch caused the winch to begin retracting. For ten seconds or so, the motor fought unsuccessfully against the trailer's structural integrity.

Eventually, with a quick tap on the brakes to assist, the motor won. The rear doors ripped away from their moorings, flew over the pickup, and slammed into the third tractor-trailer's cab, which seemed unconcerned by that happenstance. *Thank heaven for the calmness of AI-driven vehicles.*

He climbed out onto the hood and leapt forward into the trailer. Gunfire slammed into his vest as he landed, and he instinctively brought up his arms to cover his face. He let his right leg collapse and rolled to the side, behind a bunch of stacked crates attached to the wall by wide straps.

Hank grabbed and hurled all six grenades on his belt, a mix of flash-bang and stun, then drew his pistol and charged. His preference had been to bring a shotgun, but Diana had argued against it, a rare intervention on her part. He had to admit that in the tight confines of the crowded space, precision probably made more sense than random destruction. *Still, it would've been fun.*

His glasses showed heat signatures, so he knew an enemy awaited him around the next stack with another in support at a good firing angle. He rounded the corner, grabbed the person who stood there with one hand, and knocked the man's weapon out of line with the other. A torso twist assisted his prodigious strength to yank the figure into the path of the inbound rounds from his partner's rifle.

The bullets struck his captive's vest, all aimed center

mass. This was fortunate for the captive soldier and Hank, but less so for the shooter. Hank released the man as he delivered a powerful front kick, and the soldier flew backward into his partner. He drew his pistol and fired at the exposed arm of the next figure toward the front of the trailer. His opponent had entertained notions of shooting at him, but that figure jerked back out of sight.

Hank rushed forward to finish the pair he'd already interacted with. The man he'd thrown was on the floor of the truck, curled up around the likely broken bones in his chest and moaning loudly.

The other tried to align his weapon but wasn't fast enough. Hank delivered three fast punches: a jab to his foe's face, a straight punch to his sternum, and a hook to the temple. The soldier went down, either to the collective impacts or the detonation of Hank's shock gloves.

More importantly, Hank's magic reservoir increased with each punch, the power inside him building and flowing as strength through his body. The feeling made him grin, an expression that would probably make the next enemy who engaged him worry more than a little. He strode forward to find that unlucky person and ruin their day.

Diana had taken out three of the enemies in her vehicle, two with magic lightning and one with two sets of triple bullets to the vest. They all struck close enough together to cause the enemy to drop to the floor in pain. She didn't see blood, so she presumed the Kevlar had prevented penetration but that the bones underneath it had probably broken from the repeated impacts. *Serves you right.*

She took out the fourth by slamming the pallet next to him with force magic, knocking crates from the top down onto him. Her power easily ripped through the film and strap that had attempted to keep the containers secured. Two more enemies stood together at the front of the truck's storage area. She wrapped a force shield around her although she presumed they'd use anti-magic ammunition and raced ahead.

When they popped out to fire, she dropped to the floor and skidded the last several feet, rotating her body so her side crashed into the front of the truck between them. She kicked out with her heels, slamming them into the protective kneepads of the one on that side. He twisted enough to avoid having his knees bend the wrong way, but the impact still brought him down, and she thought she heard the sound of a breaking bone.

The one on the other side looked confident as he brought his weapon down toward her. That assurance vanished as her pistol sent three rounds into his left leg and another trio into his right, striking the gaps between the end of his thigh armor and the beginning of his knee protection. He went down with a scream.

She quickly tapped both of them with shock gloves to knock them out, then dug in the man's medical kit for a tourniquet and applied it to his leg. She got another from his partner's kit and did the same to the other wounded limb. Then she announced, "Major injury in here. Clock's running. Glam, send out the word."

Kayleigh replied, "Alerting the authorities now."

Above the trucks, the drone would climb higher to watch for police, emergency services, or Army response. The alert had likely gone out the moment they'd disabled the lead and tail vehicles. Diana wasn't willing to leave anything to chance if another option existed.

She'd willingly shoot a few of her enemies on sight and not shed too many tears if they died, Kevin Serrano chief among them. Soldiers doing their jobs didn't make that list. She rose to examine the stenciled number on the side of the nearest crates. "Sorting and portaling now. Wrap it up, folks."

The grenade had been a conventional one. She'd easily handled the man who'd thrown it and the rest who awaited her until only one remained. Cara hurled Demon at the man pointing a weapon at her. He flinched aside, his bullets stitching along the side of the truck and slamming into one of the crates nearby.

She shouted, "Hey, quit shooting my stuff." Her rush brought her to melee range in only a moment. In the interim, he got the barrel in line to put two rounds into her vest and another into her shoulder. She snarled a curse and reached up to slap her healing capsule, thankful he'd hit her left side.

While her flesh mended itself, she used her right hand to deliver a series of fast punches interposed with a kick to his shin and another to his knee. He was halfway to the floor when her downward punch blasted him unconscious. She shook her hand, which vibrated from the force of the impact. *That might've been a little much.*

She reached out and summoned Demon back to her grip with telekinesis and shoved the blade into its sheath. "Good here."

Hank replied, "You know, I don't think I ever imagined we'd wind up becoming thieves. Not that I have a problem with it."

His last enemy had wedged himself into an optimal position to fire on Hank's line of advance, so he pulled out his pistol and shot at the floor near the soldier, hoping for a lucky ricochet. He emptied his magazine, and as he slapped in a new one, the man fell into the space between the crates, bleeding from the legs.

Hank shook his head and muttered, "Idiot. A brave idiot, but still an idiot." He advanced, pulled out the man's medkit and gave him first-aid, then patted his foe on the shoulder after throwing his weapon to the other side of the truck. "Hang in there. Help's on the way."

He rose and quickly reviewed the stencils on the sides of the crates until he found some of the ones they were looking for. Deacon had hacked into the Army's systems to retrieve the shipment's manifest, so they knew exactly what crates were the most valuable. A fast search revealed that only one of the numbers on the list was present in his trailer. He opened a portal behind it, warned, "Incoming," and used his pent-up magic to bodily push the crate through the opening.

The warehouse on the opposite side had been secured specifically for this operation and would soon be abandoned, bereft of everything except whatever empty crates they left behind. He looked at Diana, who stood next to two stacks of boxes, and shook his head. "Should've let me bring the shotgun."

She laughed as Cara and her containers appeared in the warehouse. "All's well that ends well. Glam, are Khan and Rambo safe?"

The tech's annoyed voice replied, "Of course."

Diana nodded. "Good. Then let's see what goodies the Army has involuntarily donated to our cause today."

CHAPTER THREE

S loan forced himself up off the long couch, which was worn and threadbare in places. It gave off a faint scent of smoke and not the kind from tobacco. The apartment on the north side of Pittsburgh was one of several in a building that was half housing and half artists' workspaces. It featured a large room that included the kitchen, living room, and dining room.

The rest of the space was limited to a small bathroom and a bedroom only big enough for the bed inside it. High windows with old curtains covered the outer wall, and a couple of beat-up tables and chairs finished the furniture.

Deacon had thought the location would be appropriate for his current cover. After seeing his neighbors over the last day or two, Sloan couldn't disagree. *A little bigger wouldn't have been bad.* The techs had wired the place for surveillance before he moved in, and he waved at a camera as he headed for the rack of clothes in the corner.

He possessed a limited wardrobe for the current operation, simple stuff appropriate to his cover as a salesperson of all trades. For today's outing to a local bar to see what information he could pick up, he selected khakis, a polo shirt, and a leather jacket that was far less cool than what he would ordinarily wear. He went with hiking boots rather than combat-inspired ones. After changing, he walked through the apartment for the first time in his new identity. *Chuck Waserman. Nice to meet you.*

As he strode down the steep stairs from the fourth floor to ground level and out into the fairly hip neighborhood, he continued practicing the lines he would use when he met people, getting his head into the new persona. Deacon and Kayleigh had put together a fictitious paper trail and history for the identity, but none of them expected anyone to look at it. The current disguise wasn't going to be used to move against the government or other folks who would engage in computer investigation of his background. He had a different quarry in his sights.

People were out on the streets, walking, talking, driving, and creating hazardous situations by keeping their noses in their cell phones. He passed several coffee shops with outdoor seating, although the chill in the air meant that only a hardy few occupied them. He flipped up his collar and buttoned the top fastener of his jacket with a shiver.

The walk to his destination took him through the hip community he lived in, then through a far more gentrified version of it where the coffees cost twice as much, and each came with a design in the foam. The baristas here—or what back in the day would be called servers—would no doubt consider themselves artists of the highest caliber. *Who's to say they're not? I certainly can't make any recognizable designs in foam or any other medium. That kind of stuff takes talent and training.*

The thought was half Chuck's and half Sloan's. By the time he reached the older neighborhood, one that involved steep hills in every direction and small houses placed uncomfortably close together, he was fully in Chuck's mind. He assessed everything he passed, calculating if there might be a way to pull a profit from it. He nodded at those he encountered with a genuine-looking smile gracing his lips. *You never know who could be your next customer or supplier.*

After another ten minutes of walking, he arrived at his destination. The Sleeping Leprechaun bar occupied a corner lot. There were no windows on the ground level to break the monotony of the dusky red painted slabs of wood that made up its façade. On the second and third stories, windows with curtains suggested apartments.

He pulled open the building's front door and walked from late afternoon into night. The interior was dark, moody, and entirely unpretentious. He almost expected to see sawdust on the floor—the tavern had that sort of "old" feel.

Tables with booths ran along the walls to the left and right, and a jukebox at the far end played Celtic music with lots of banjo. A bar mimicked the shape of the outer walls, with the point where it made a ninety-degree turn aimed at the door. He sauntered to an unoccupied space toward the right, far enough from the entrance not to be noticed, and slid onto a stool. The bar's surface was old wood, cracked and gouged, its dark wood pitted with lighter sections. *No one would slide a glass on this thing for fear of dousing their customer in beer.*

Two bartenders worked behind the wooden barrier, both females between twenty-five and forty in his initial estimation. By the end of the night, after watching them move and act, he'd have a much better idea of their age and probably some insight into their backgrounds. The bar didn't have a uniform since one of them wore dark jeans and a bright red blouse that dipped dangerously far in the front, and the other a black tank top that occasionally rode up to display the top of her leather pants and the bottom of her toned abs. That was the one working on his side of the place.

He took note of the straight, long black hair pulled into a ponytail behind her. She wore dangly earrings and makeup dramatic enough to be notable in the bar's dim light, especially her red lips. She offered him a professional smile. "What'll you have?"

"Sam Adams. Draft if you've got it. Bottle's fine if not."

"Bottle it is." She walked toward a cooler set under the bar, and he used the opportunity to perform a more considered survey of the place. He'd noticed the frames on the walls when he'd entered but hadn't identified the subjects, which were notable in themselves. Each showed an image of some part of the steelmaking process, Pittsburgh's history hanging as a reminder of what the town had once been. The art was well-executed, not photographs but high-quality artist's representations that seemed almost photographic.

The bar had a blue-collar vibe to it, but he also detected another atmosphere, the one he was hoping to find. It was present in the woman who handed the beer to him, her heavy wooden bracelet *clinking* against the bottle. It was evident in the way people leaned over to talk surreptitiously across the tables that separated the booths as if they didn't want their voices to carry.

The clientele was a mix of magical and non-magical, primarily witches and wizards to his eye. The arcane clientele kept its presence subtle but didn't exactly hide it, either. He imagined many of the people who came in would be aware it was a place frequented by magicals. *Which is why I'm here.*

The bartender said, "Two bucks," and he handed over three.

"That cheap?"

"New customer special."

He laughed. "You're good."

She gave a small eye roll. "Our business is pretty much made up of regulars. Not too hard to notice when someone you don't know comes in."

He offered her a smile. "Well, let's fix that. I'm Chuck. Chuck Waserman."

She stuck out her hand, the one without the bracelet. "Jackie."

"Good to meet you, Jackie."

"Likewise. New to the north side?"

He nodded. "New to town. Looking to drum up some business."

She leaned against the bar and ran a palm across her forehead. "What's your field?" The place was empty enough that she wasn't ignoring any other patrons quite yet, although a few had entered during the short time they'd been speaking.

Sloan laughed. "Little of this, little of that. I help people get things they want, help other people sell stuff they don't want, and do my best to grease the wheels for those with enough money not to want to do it themselves."

She shook her head. "Sounds like a difficult hustle."

"Not as hard as bartending. Been there, didn't have what it took."

Jackie looked out over the space behind him. "This place is pretty good. Not too rowdy, and when things get a little out of hand, customers tend to police their own." She knocked a knuckle on the bar. "Enjoy your drink. I've got to get back to it."

He couldn't help watching as she walked away. She was slender and attractive, and the leather pants fit her well. *No way she's going to be interested in Chuck, though. Too old, too boring. Story of my life.*

Sloan spent the next hour nursing his beer and the one that followed it, surreptitiously angling his watch at different tables and clusters of people around the room. Hidden inside his timepiece was a directional mic that fed the comm in his ear. The technology electronically eliminated the background sound and amplified whatever he pointed it at.

He heard a bunch of stuff that wasn't at all interesting, complaints about work, gripes about the cost of potion materials, and gossip about the rich neighborhood nearby. One pair of men talked in rather crude terms about the bartender in the red blouse until she came over and told them with a smattering of colorful vulgarities to knock it off or she'd throw them out the front door herself.

He was about ready to leave when a trio of women walked in, dressed in black and covered in dramatic goth makeup. He would've considered them posers if not for the sense of magical power that radiated from them. They had some spells active.

Sloan pointed the watch at them and listened as they ordered drinks, then tracked them as they headed over to a booth. Their decision to order at the bar and carry their beverages to their seats rather than making the bartenders come out suggested they might be regulars. The familiar way they slipped into the booth supported that conclusion.

Finally, he heard the news he'd been waiting for. It wasn't what he wanted to hear, not by a long shot. However, it suggested his presence in Pittsburgh was a good thing. One witch said to the others, "I got a message from our fearless leader." The other two snorted at that. She continued, "Vivienne has gone missing. That's three months in a row we've lost someone around the same set of dates."

Sloan kept the frown from reaching his lips as he threw a five-dollar bill on the bar as a parting tip. He waved and called, "See you next time, Jackie." She returned the gesture, and he headed for the exit. *Going to have to get into some police records and maybe find out some stuff that's not in the computer systems. Fortunately, I know who to ask for an assist.*

CHAPTER FOUR

Diana was seated in the main room of Ruby's bunker, reclined comfortably on the couch she'd spent far too much time on of late. The loss of their base on Bannerman's Island banged around inside her brain, a source of constant frustration. It made her want to find Kevin Serrano and punch him in the head repeatedly, like one of those old inflatable clown toys that kids used to beat on as an early introduction to the joys of violence.

The knowledge that she and her team couldn't stay in Ruby's stronghold any longer enhanced her attitudinal challenge. Doing so risked Serrano training his attention on Ruby, which was entirely unacceptable. The leader of the Mist Elves wouldn't bat an eyelash at that threat, but Diana believed it was too much to ask. *Better that this place serves as a refuge if things go wrong rather than as our primary location.*

Her team surrounded her, except Sloan, who was virtually present by comm. Rath sat on her left, Cara on her right. Hank leaned against a wall across the room, and

Bryant, who was still healing but mostly back to normal, occupied the chair he'd used since his capture and subsequent rescue.

Their other walking wounded, Tony, occupied the other soft chair in the room, finally back from the hospital. His movements were far more awkward than usual, a sign that his pain continued, but he'd assured her privately that his ability to shoot was unaffected, and thus he was ready to go. *That's one of the problems with leading a bunch of confident, high-spirited people. You can't make them take care of themselves.*

The sarcastic voice inside her head replied, "Oh, and you wouldn't know anything about that."

Shut it. Deacon and Kayleigh were present as well, sharing an overstuffed chair. Deacon was in the seat and Kayleigh perched on the arm, slightly overlapping her boyfriend. Those two had proven their value again and again, as had all her team members.

Pride swelled inside her at what fundamentally amazing people she led. She coughed to cover the emotional moment. "Okay, Hank. Tell everyone what we took from the Army."

He rubbed a hand over his bald head. "Well, we got most of what we hoped to obtain. One of the numbers Deacon provided wasn't on the trucks, or we missed it. I blame Cara."

Diana's second-in-command replied nonchalantly, "Screw you, muscle head."

The big man chuckled and continued, "We got a little something for everybody. For Deacon and Kayleigh, several advanced drones."

Rath asked, "With caltrops?"

Everybody laughed, and Kayleigh replied, "That'll be our first modification, buddy. Promise."

He nodded happily and patted the head of the dog beside him, Max. The Borzoi had been sleeping on the couch for the last half-hour, completely undisturbed by her team assembling around him. *Probably thinks they're all here to see him.*

Hank went on, "For Tony, Kayleigh, and Anik, some advanced medkits. They have artificial intelligence on board, automatic deployment of meds and such, really good. It will take some time to figure out how to use them properly, but they should give a nice sense of security to our people who can't rely on healing potions."

Diana asked, "And for the rest of us?"

He gave her a fake frown. "Tone it down there, boss, I'm getting to it. We get one thing that's a little useful, but not really, and another that's totally useful. We're the proud owners of several crates of M320 under-barrel grenade launchers."

"I hate those," Tony complained.

Cara countered, "They're not *that* bad."

Hank lifted a hand. "There are as many opinions on the M203 replacement as there are people to give them. That's not important. You want the three-twenty, use it. You want to stick with the two-oh-three, which is what I'm going to do, do that.

"What's most important is that they came with a bunch of experimental grenade types. So, the techs get some to reverse engineer them, and so do Ruby and her mentor Margrave, for the same purpose. Hopefully, before too long, we'll have some cool new options to wreak havoc on Serrano and his men and women."

Rath added, "And drones."

Deacon countered, "Right. And, the way things are going, probably some of those dancing robot dogs that now have sniper rifles mounted on them that we'll inevitably face."

Diana scowled at him. "Well, I see we're all in an optimistic mood today."

"Having that prick Serrano kick us out of our base, *again*, has that effect, boss," Kayleigh noted.

"I get it. I *feel* it. That's why we're changing our plans again. We can't risk using this place as a base of operations anymore. It can be a refuge, but not our primary." Nods greeted her words.

"So, we'll split up. We can probably expect that Serrano's going to be annoyed at the message I left for him, so we should keep our heads down for a while. Deacon, any news on the little present we left with the video?"

The infomancer sighed. "Yeah. Their people were too good and blocked the worm from getting in. They tried to turn it back on me, but fortunately I'm *also* too good. I'm feeding them misinformation at the moment. They'll see through it eventually and try something else in return. It's a game we infomancers like to play."

Diana shrugged. "As expected. Would've been nice if it had worked out, but we're no worse off for trying than we would've been otherwise. Anyway, we'll use the buddy system wherever possible. Cara and Anik, you're together. Tony, you're with Hank. Sloan stays in Pittsburgh, and Bryant plans to do something stupid."

Her boyfriend and nominal superior replied, "Hey. I'm right here."

"You say that like I haven't already told you this to your face repeatedly."

"Still. Where's the love?"

A couple of catcalls sounded in response to the comment, and Diana shook her head in faux despair. Sloan said, "Everyone knows what I'm doing up in Pittsburgh, looking into the church that Rath's friends thought might be suspicious. What's your objective?"

Bryant replied, "I've been reviewing this whole thing in my head, over and over. Something about it doesn't smell right. We're only seeing part of the game, whatever it is. It could be because the rest is hidden, or it could be because we don't have the right vantage point at the moment. I want to try to discover what we don't know before it lands right on our heads."

Deacon offered, "Might be safer to hack stuff. Maybe breaking into the White House servers would be less dangerous than that plan."

Diana tipped her head in his direction. "See? I'm not the only one who thinks you're an idiot, Bryant."

He shrugged. "I have contacts. People whose loyalty I think I can still trust."

"*Think* being the operative word there," Cara pointed out.

"Acknowledged. Believe me. I'll take every precaution."

Diana sighed. "It's not like you'd listen if we told you not to, anyway."

He leaned back regally. "Sometimes it's good to be king."

Tony remarked, "Royalty has a history of winding up deposed and or beheaded. Try to avoid that. Especially the second one."

Everyone chuckled at that comment, and Diana took over the conversation again. "Our troublesome technological twosome will stick together. They'll coordinate everyone's actions, ensure communication flows, and give us all support in the field. Plus, they'll keep an eye on the Network."

Rath corrected, "Trollnet."

Kayleigh frowned. "Like Skynet?"

He laughed. "Only not quite as murderous."

Diana shook her head. "I'm not sure that one has staying power, but sure, it'll work for now. They'll watch over the Trollnet. So, Sloan's in Pittsburgh, and Bryant will be messing around in D.C., trying to lose his head.

"Cara and Anik, you're headed to the Big Easy. I want you to get to New Orleans tomorrow and keep a low profile. Don't show your faces at the Drunken Dragons, for instance. Route any communication to Zeb through the Trollnet and arrange meetings that way. We have to get started on figuring out what the hell Maîtresse Mambo Severine Eschete is up to."

They both nodded, and Cara asked, "What are we doing for money?"

Kayleigh waved a hand airily. "Rob a bank, blow up an ATM. You'll figure it out."

Diana replied, "No, Kayleigh and Deacon will do their jobs and keep cracking poorly secured government lines of cash and credit. We'll figure something else out, eventually.

For now, what our former bosses don't know won't hurt them."

She shifted her gaze to her next targets. "Tony and Hank, your job will be to find us temporary bases in Pittsburgh, D.C., and New Orleans, on the assumption that we'll have to operate locally at some point. Plus, find us a couple of other locations to act as storage. Deacon and Kayleigh can help with rentals, dealing with the money trail, etcetera."

They both agreed to her orders, but she saw a glint in Hank's eye. Frankly, she was surprised it had taken so long to appear. "Hank. Stay away from the bus."

He scowled, "But, this is the perfect—

He'd been in love with the mobile armory since the day he thought it up. She countered darkly, "Hank."

He sighed and crossed his arms. "Fine. But you're making a mistake."

Bryant replied, "Wouldn't be her first. Speaking of which, what do *you* plan to do while everyone else is off obeying your orders?"

Diana closed her eyes and shook her head. "Nylotte has gotten the idea that I owe her for helping us out. With Tony, among other things. So, Rath and I are going to pay that bill."

CHAPTER FIVE

S loan wore a different disguise today. He'd temporarily set Chuck Waserman aside. This one made him appear twenty years older and included a walking stick that was decoration rather than utility for his character. He didn't expect to be intercepted or even noticed with electronic surveillance. Still, the clientele of the business he was heading to visit was traditionally moneyed, and of CEO age, so the persona was appropriate.

He walked down the long, narrow street, peering in shop windows on his side of the road. Pittsburgh's Strip District was historically a place where truckers dropped off deliveries overnight, and businesses visited in the early hours to take care of their wholesale shopping. Now, it was much more directly consumer-friendly and thus livelier, with shops and stores of every kind. One in particular drew a smile, a stall selling unlicensed fan gear for the local sports teams, t-shirts making fun of their nearest neighbors in Cleveland and Baltimore.

Sloan took a couple of turns, abandoning the main drag

for a more industrial lane, and found the business he was looking for. It showed a pair of slightly overlapped circles, like a partial Venn diagram, with "Two Worlds Security" emblazoned underneath it. He pulled open the door and walked into the cramped entry area, which was quite familiar.

Diana had created the place as a cover operation when her team's base was in Pittsburgh. No one was in the receiving room, which wasn't a surprise. It was too small for anything other than a reception desk, and he wouldn't spend his time in it voluntarily, either.

The interior door opened and James Maxis, known to Diana's team as Starsky, entered the room. "May I help you?" His dark hair had always pushed regulation length and was now down to his shoulders, but he was still clean-shaven and looked even more fit than he had while in uniform.

Waiting until the door had fully closed behind him, Sloan straightened, dropping the posture portion of his camouflage, and laughed. "Well, I hope so, Starsky, or why the hell did I come here?"

The man blinked several times, then broke into a grin. "Damn, you are *good* at the disguise thing. Sloan, long time no see." He strode forward and extended a hand, which Sloan shook warmly. "What can I do for you?"

Sloan gestured with his chin toward the main part of the building. "Can you lock up for a bit? I wouldn't want to have our conversation interrupted."

The other man laughed. "Of course. We don't get that much walk-in traffic." He moved to do as Sloan had asked.

"Business is good?"

The lock *clicked*, and Maxis turned back. "Very good. We've retired completely from the force, even the contracted gigs we'd been taking on. Added a few underlings, but they don't work out of here. Hutch is going to be really excited to see you."

Sloan followed the other man into the rear of the building, which had previously held the team's modular training equipment. Now that the gear was elsewhere, it was a wide-open area with a corner remodeled into a decent workspace housing a few desks.

Vicki Green rose from behind her desk. Her long blonde hair was in a ponytail rather than in the bun she'd worn while on the force, and her tank top showed muscular arms that matched her fit form. She skipped over and hugged Sloan, then punched him hard in the arm.

He rubbed the injured spot and spoke with wounded dignity, "Ow. What did I do to deserve that?"

She put her hands on her hips. "You don't call. You don't write. You don't visit for like a year." She shook her head. "Perhaps you need to look up the word 'friend' in a dictionary." Her smile took the venom from her words, and she gestured for him to sit at an empty desk.

He complied, and after Maxis sat beside him, said, "I want to hire you two for a little work."

Starsky quipped, "Cash up front. You're a fugitive. A ronin. We can't trust you."

Sloan laughed. "Untrue. You've never seen my face on TV."

"Only because you're a mystery man. But your name is out there," Green replied.

He put a hand on his chest. "*I* am Winston Thurston

Howell the Ninth. Surely the government is not looking for *me*." Another round of laughter greeted his words.

Starsky asked, "Seriously, what do you need?"

All the humor left Sloan's voice. "We're tracking a cult, one that seems obsessed with Rhazdon artifacts."

Green observed, "They're muscling into your turf because of *your* obsession with the damn things?"

He shrugged. "That's probably a legitimate way of looking at the situation. Long story short, though, these people seem to have a penchant for human sacrifice. Well, magical sacrifice."

The pair straightened in their chairs. Neither was magical, but both were devoted to justice and only slightly less to law and order. Green said, "Details?"

Sloan shrugged. "Rumor is they've taken a church on the north side as their base. I've confirmed that, at least somewhat. Before I start digging in, I need information on whether there have been missing persons associated with that area or only in town. Both the ones that will be on the books and those that won't."

Maxis frowned. "You think they'll be missing from the system because they're magicals?"

Sloan shook his head. "I'm not throwing any stones here. For all we know, the people vanishing could be homeless or might be unreported for some other reason. That sort of thing. You were on the streets long enough to know the drill. Not all the relevant information makes it into the computer systems. If it did, we wouldn't ever need human intelligence for anything, with infomancers on the payroll."

They both nodded, and Green replied, "We're on it. Let us know how to contact you."

That day, Sloan had exited the way he'd come in. However, being inside had allowed him to refresh his memory of viable portal destinations within the building. When the pair called him back a few days later and invited him to visit, he simply created a rift between his apartment and the office and strode from one to the other.

Maxis stood in front of a fancy coffee maker, hopefully brewing some, and Green was next to an old-style bulletin board, snatching pages off a nearby printer and pinning them to the cork surface with bright red push pins. Sloan grabbed a chair and pulled it over near her, then accepted a mug from her partner. "Thanks for the coffee and for whatever you've discovered. Let's have it."

Maxis said, "We're so good that you're gonna want to pay us double."

The joke seemed forced, but Sloan gave it a short laugh and a nod. "Hacked government lines of credit for everybody. Seriously, spill."

Green pinned a large map to the board, one with circles centered on the church Rath's contacts had identified drawn on it. She gestured at it. "Inner ring, no reported missing persons. Probably keeping their nearest area clean."

Maxis added, "That's fairly typical serial killer behavior. Doesn't usually help them all that much, but provides a sense of security."

Green continued, "Next ring out, six missing persons cases in the last two months. A pair of reports specified magicals, but as you know, that information doesn't always get captured."

Sloan nodded. "The next ring?"

Maxis growled, "Eleven. Seven magical for sure."

The final ring was larger, including more space. "And the outer?"

Green replied, "Eighteen and twelve."

Sloan frowned at the dire news. "But no bodies?"

She shrugged, seeming as unhappy as he felt in the face of the discoveries. "A few here and there, which we presume were people who went missing the normal ways."

Maxis growled, "*Normal*. As if lives ending by violence is in any way normal."

Sloan agreed but couldn't let the conversation fall off track. "Logically, when magicals kill people, the bodies often won't be found. The World In Between is good for that." He shuddered at the thought of that chaotic dimension accessible only by magic. "So, that's rather more than I expected you'd find."

Green replied, "I have all the reports here, and we can pin them up and look for similarities and such later. We also talked to some old contacts, and they all have the feeling something is definitely up. Without prompting, they mentioned both the north side and magicals."

He sighed. "I knew that was going to be the answer, but somehow, I *really* hoped it wouldn't be."

The pair nodded in unison. "Same here," Green replied.

Maxis said, "Tell us how we can help. No charge."

Sloan rose, frustration forcing him into motion. "Keep

working your contacts. See if you can find out anything more, like where these people might've been seen in the days before they vanished. That sort of thing. You know the drill. Try to narrow down an area in space and a window in time for me. Then I'll go in and see what's what."

The other man observed, "Sounds dangerous."

He nodded. "Yeah. By all evidence, these people are twisted as hell. Makes me nauseous just thinking about it, really."

"Give us a few days. We'll get you everything there is to find," Green confirmed.

"Thank you." Sloan opened a portal back to his apartment, where he could lie in his rented bed and talk with the rest of the team over the comm about how to approach the situation. Maybe he could get the feeling of horror in his belly to subside. *Clearly, there's only one way this works. I'm going to have to get inside.*

CHAPTER SIX

Sloan was back in his Chuck Waserman identity, which was becoming a comfortable brain to live in. Chuck didn't worry too much about anything other than the next job, the next payday. He pulled on the door of the bar he'd been frequenting of late. A blast of heat hit him through the opening.

It had taken Starsky and Hutch two days to find an area of interest based on the last known locations of a cluster of people who'd disappeared. As soon as he had the information, he'd cased the neighborhoods the data had highlighted, looking with an experienced eye for something that seemed to fit as a likely pickup site.

He found it in The Mill, a bar that boasted a hefty magical clientele. He'd spent part of each day inside its walls over the last week and occasionally multiple times, watching, listening, and generally being present. He played his role, making supposed business calls from the bar, holding down a table to do paperwork and other appropriate tasks to support his cover.

Sloan knew from his nightly check-ins with the rest of the team that they were all pursuing the assignments Diana had given them, moving slowly and cautiously for fear that Kevin Serrano and his people might pop up around any given corner to capture them. It was a weird time and circumstance for his situation to be more stable than the others.

He smiled at the bartender, a wizard with an impressive white beard that he kept braided so it wouldn't get into the drinks. The man slid a beer to him without asking as Sloan sat at the long bar that covered one wall. Unlike the Sleeping Leprechaun, this tavern was well maintained, probably through a mix of magic and muscle power. The ceiling lights were dim, but the bar had chandeliers over it, and each table along the walls had a small lamp resting on it.

He sipped the drink, a local lager that didn't hit too hard, and twisted in his chair to look at the other patrons in the bar as he always did. In his cover as an intermediary who thrived on making connections between buyers and sellers, it was logical for him to check out the evening's possibilities. Over the past week, he'd identified several people who could conceivably be part of the cult or might at least be acting on its behalf.

Two possibles were male and the other female. It was the woman whose involvement he was most certain of. She occupied her usual spot, a table far from the door with a glass of red wine in front of her. Her bright blonde hair fell over her face as she leaned forward, speaking earnestly to a man in the opposite booth. Sloan had concluded she was a magical based primarily on gut instincts. He trusted those intuitions when they arrived.

He'd gotten flashes of insight, his particular magical talent, on several of the other regulars, but not on her. Her body language always seemed as if she was presenting an argument, trying to convince her conversational partner of something. The woman consistently had a hand raised to shield her mouth so he couldn't read her lips, and he wasn't about to use the directional mic in this place.

He was too close to his quarry, and if she was indeed a true lead, she might be looking out for such things. He didn't want to risk spooking her. So, all he could do was watch and collect information as innocuously as possible.

The people she'd spoken with had been exclusively male, and he'd flashed on one of those. The magical moment had told him the man had elf in his blood and a chip on his shoulder about how others treated magicals. With that insight to guide him, Sloan had looked for similar indications in the others she talked to and had noticed that they, too, often seemed angry or irritated.

He didn't imagine it was from a conversation with the woman. The blonde hair complemented perfect makeup, and one couldn't help but admire her wardrobe, which was universally form-fitting, currently a beige sweater and ripped blue jeans. He finished his drink and slid the glass back to the wizard, who rapidly replaced it with another. Sloan punched some buttons on his phone and lifted it to his ear.

On the other end, Kayleigh's voice replied, "Italian kitchen, home of the gnocchi as big as your head. What can we get you?"

Sloan laughed. "I was wondering about your catering prices."

"What kind of event?"

"Small party."

Kayleigh dropped the fictional part of the conversation. "No new information on that matter, sorry."

He nodded and kept a smile plastered on his face. "As expected." She meant that Deacon hadn't been able to find anything on the woman Sloan was watching, despite the many pictures he'd sent back, taken from his display glasses. "Let me know if anything changes. Oh, and you should consider taking reservations."

Kayleigh laughed. "Nope. First come, first served. Line forms an hour before opening."

He shook his head. "Thanks for nothing. See you."

The wizard, who had approached during his call, asked, "Good news?"

Sloan let out a soft groan. "My sister. She works for an Italian restaurant and doesn't want me coming by."

The man raised an eyebrow. "Did you do something to offend her?"

He snorted. "Yeah. I exist."

"I have a sister like that."

"She one of your kind?"

He nodded. "A witch. It's in the blood, like they say."

The bartender ambled off, and Sloan continued watching the woman. The man she'd been talking to departed with a smile. *Guess I might as well push this thing forward.* He rose and walked over to her table. "May I join you for a second?"

44

She looked at him dubiously, then shrugged. "Free country."

He took the seat and asked, "Get you a drink?"

She shook her head. "I've reached my limit. About time for me to hit the road."

"I've seen you in here before."

She nodded. "I've seen you, seeing me."

He laughed. "Surely, men being interested in you isn't a new experience."

She smiled, but it was less flirty than suspicious. "The blonde hair does seem to attract more than my fair share of weirdos."

He put a hand on his chest. "First, ouch, and second, you got me. I'm definitely a weirdo. I'm Chuck Waserman."

"Lila."

"I wanted to talk to you because it seems like you know a lot of folks. I'm in the business of people, of making connections, helping a person who needs one thing find someone who can supply it, that sort of deal." He drew a card from his shirt pocket and slipped it over to her. "As such, networking is important. As I said, you seem to know a lot of people."

She took the business card and reviewed it, then gave him a raised eyebrow over top of it. "Are you suggesting I'm promiscuous, Mr. Waserman?"

Sloan laughed. "Not at all. I don't judge, and I don't make assumptions. I know from seeing you here that you know people. Maybe they're folks I'd like to know, too. I gave my card out to a few others here and in the other bars I frequent. Always looking for my next friend."

She nodded, seeming to buy the story. "Business friend, or pleasure friend?"

"Primarily the first, but quite open to the second, if there's chemistry." Her body language indicated that she was disinclined to stay much longer, so he rose. "Maybe I'll catch you around another time. Take care. I have one more person I need to talk to before I can call it a night." He turned and headed for the other end of the bar, where a regular he hadn't met sat at a corner table.

He repeated the scene on a couple of successive nights, making superficial conversation with Lila while appearing to do the job he'd claimed to have. After three days, one of which ended without her appearance, he was beginning to think he'd have to do something more obvious to make the connection. Then he caught a break.

He was holding down his normal seat when an elf came into the bar, one with the slender form, sharp features, and pointed ears that made him impossible to misidentify. He requested wine and seemed frazzled. Sloan ventured, "Having a rough one?"

The other man laughed. "You could say that. I was enjoying myself at the casino when a bunch of drunk morons decided it was 'pick on an elf' day."

Sloan scowled. "Assholes. Did you blast them into next week? I would've."

The elf gave him a dour look. "Nah. Around here, that's a good way to end up in jail. Or the morgue. Drunk Pittsburghers like to fight and don't know when to stop. I have a problem with the latter sometimes myself."

He chuckled. "Sounds like drunk people everywhere, to be honest, at least the ones who are scumbags to begin with." When the elf finished his wine, Sloan bought him another round, and they continued talking about the ill-treatment of magicals in the world in general.

Sloan knew the treatment was no more or less awful than that experienced by many other groups, but since his target had arrived at the bar halfway through their conversation, he played it up. Finally, he wrapped up his talk with the elf and headed out, waving at the woman as he went.

His instincts proved correct when she joined him outside a few minutes later. She looked around, then spotted him leaning on the wall, feigning intoxication. She asked, "You okay?"

He laughed. "World got a little spinny there for a second. I think I had one drink too many with that elf at the bar. He had a bad day."

She nodded. "Seemed like it bothered you."

Sloan snorted. "Of course it bothers me. Magicals have as much right to be here as non-magicals, and every magical has as much right as any other magical or human to not be discriminated against."

She stepped closer and said quietly, "I happen to have some friends who think the same way you do. We get together now and again for a chat. Next gathering is tomorrow night. Interested in joining us?"

He grinned. "Are you trying to pull me into some pyramid scheme, or are you asking me out on a date?"

She laughed. "A little from column A, a little from column B, maybe."

"Okay. I'm in, either way."

She pulled out his card, which she'd been carrying, scrawled a phone number on the back, and returned it to him. "Call me tomorrow at noon. I'll let you know when and where to show up."

He grinned. His inner self was as happy at the potential for a way into whatever the woman was a part of as his outer self appeared to be at the prospect of a date with her. "You're on."

CHAPTER SEVEN

The garage area of Kevin Serrano's base was busier than ever before. New personnel had arrived, along with their gear and some additional equipment his team had requisitioned. Sorting them out and organizing teams was his challenge at the moment.

Across the expanse, his second-in-command, Natasha Kline, was doing much the same thing he was, pointing, answering questions, and ordering people to do things. He clapped a new arrival on the shoulder and directed him toward the locker room, then shook his head and crossed to his partner.

As he arrived, Tash laughed at him. "You look a little flustered there, boss."

He gave her a playful scowl. "When I said we needed more people and more things, I didn't mean *all* the people and things."

She shrugged. "What can I say? Your staff is effective, efficient, and enthusiastic."

He shook his head. "You also seem to have overestimated how much space we have."

"Most of these folks are only here for a layover. They'll be deployed into the field to look for cult activity like you ordered."

He nodded. "And, not incidentally, to watch out for Sheen and her team."

"Of course." She took a step closer and lowered her voice. "What about Bradford and his rental mercenaries?"

Kevin sighed. Hiring Bradford's team had *not* been one of the more successful parts of his current assignment. "Ace in the hole, at this point. I'd prefer not to rely on them again unless it's vital to a particular operation for some reason."

Tash nodded, seemingly satisfied. "Well, we certainly have plenty of people, no doubt about that. The question is, where do we send them?"

"Let's go talk to Cassandra and see what her folks have found." Tash followed him through the halls of their office building until they reached the main technical center, an oversized space with monitors of various sizes covering one wall and two semicircular desks filled with technicians facing them. The woman in charge of this area was one of the better infomancers he'd ever worked with. More importantly, she was also highly competent in all sorts of other areas, including managing the folks around her. He called, "Cass, a word?"

She took off her headset and set it on the desk, then rose and crossed to them. "Busy day, boss."

Kevin nodded. "We're just getting started, really. Pretty soon, though, Tash will have to stack new arrivals one on top of another in the storage rooms because we're out of space. I hope you've identified some places to send them?"

"We have. A unit will go to New York to take one more look at the place we know Sheen's team hit. Another should head to New Orleans because of the rumors we know our enemies are investigating. If it's enough for them, it's enough for us.

"One to Vegas because any kind of cult would fit in there. That group will also cover Magic City. That's less about finding the cult and more about finding Sheen, of course."

Tash nodded. "I'd recommend separate teams for Sin City and Ely. Ruby Achera also bears watching. She's been thick with Sheen since their first meeting, as near as we can tell."

Cass shrugged. "Like you said, we have lots of people. We can do that."

Kevin said, "Tell me more about New Orleans," but a moment later, all of them were distracted by an image that appeared on the big monitor. It showed feeds from their drones that routinely flew over Washington, but now it displayed the parking area outside the building's front door. That in itself wasn't notable, but the two large Army trucks that had pulled up were.

Tash said, "What the hell? Were you expecting a visit and forgot to tell me, boss?"

Kevin shook his head. "Comes as a surprise to me, too. Let's go see what they want." As he led the way out of the computer center, he unconsciously squeezed his left arm against his torso, verifying the pistol in the shoulder holster was where it belonged.

The orders from his oversight committee forced him to rely on the Army for this operation. He'd never fully trusted them, or more specifically, didn't fully trust the leaders, Major Leland and Colonel Nance, who seemed to have an agenda of their own. *Well, I suppose that's not unexpected since they're using us as a testing ground for their new magical military units. Still, I wouldn't trust them as far as Cassandra could throw them, which isn't far.*

The two vehicles had parked in front of the main door. The one to the right had ejected a pair of soldiers in dress uniforms, a man and a woman. Both held the rank of lieutenant, and both were blond, short-haired, and modestly built. The woman stuck out a hand to him. "Mr. Serrano. I'm Halston, and this is Ames. We're here to provide technical assistance to your computer people and infomancers."

Tash said, casually but with an edge if you knew to listen for it, "I don't recall us requesting that sort of support."

The man shrugged. "We have our orders, Ms. Kline. You can take it up with our superiors if you want. In the meantime, we have more people and a lot of gear in the back. Where would you like us to set up?"

Kevin replied, "Go ahead and get it inside, first left, second right. There's an unoccupied space adjacent to our current tech center you can use. Work with Cassandra, connect how she tells you to."

The woman nodded. "Will do, sir." They both turned together, literally in unison, to head back to the truck. He found their similarities strange. He muttered, only loud enough for Tash to hear, "Cloning, you think?"

A snort escaped her. "Could be. Could also be lots of

training and working closely. Sometimes partners come to resemble each other, like old married folks." She tilted her head to the left. "More trouble, ten o'clock."

He turned the direction she indicated to the vehicle parked on that side. It ejected five soldiers in combat fatigues, carrying khaki duffel bags that looked heavy. One of them got out ahead of the others and stopped in front of him. "Compliments of Major Leland, sir. We're a fully qualified magical unit, seconded to your command."

Tash asked, "Are you capable?"

The man turned his head to her and grinned. "Highly."

His second-in-command's nostrils flared as though the statement had bothered her, but she didn't reply. Kevin said, "All right. Get your gear together, grab some food, then we'll send you out to the field. Might as well get you right to work."

"Affirmative, sir." When they left, he turned to Tash. "What's up?"

She shook her head. "Something off about that one. His," she waved as if she couldn't quite describe it, "aura, for lack of a better word. It's weird."

He said, as quietly as he could, "Think he has an artifact? Could that do it?"

She nodded. "That was my first guess. Which makes him either very strong and capable or a lunatic who's convinced everyone he's not one. He'll bear watching. Where are you thinking of sending them?"

"New Orleans. Seems like the place where we've gotten the best leads so far."

She sighed. "Sure, sure. Here I am, toiling away to make

things run around here, and you're granting those five an all-expenses-paid vacation."

"So that's your idea of a good time, is it?"

"Music, drinks, and interesting people everywhere? You know it."

He grinned. "Well, then, you'll like the next part of the plan. You're headed to NOLA, too."

CHAPTER EIGHT

One of the team's magicals opened a portal for Tash to cross from D.C. to New Orleans, and she stepped through it, hefting the large backpack she wore over both her shoulders. The arrival spot was a couple of blocks away from the French Quarter. She walked casually in that direction, enjoying the warmth and sun, so different from winter in the District of Columbia. "It might be a working vacation, but damn, this isn't half bad."

Her phone's GPS fed a map inside her sunglasses, guiding her to the meeting with her local contact. She took several turns after entering the Quarter and finally found the place, an apartment above a touristy voodoo shop. She climbed the stairs and knocked on the door. The person she'd expected to see opened it.

He was bearded, dark-skinned, and curly black hair flowed down past his shoulders. He stepped back to let her in and spread his arms wide. "Literally the best available property in the Quarter. No, don't thank me, just doing my job and being excellent at it, as usual."

Tash laughed. "You're ridiculous, Chance. But you did come through, no question."

He chuckled. "Have to take the good with the bad, right? You look a little tired, by the way."

She'd taken off her sunglasses, which must've been the inspiration for his comment. She scowled. "Jerk."

Chance laughed again. "Honesty *is* one of my best qualities. You know that, T."

She nodded. "I do, true that."

He walked down a short hallway and turned right. She followed and entered a small kitchen. He popped the caps on two bottles of Abita Amber beer pulled from the fridge and handed one to her. She took a long drink and sighed. "Now it feels like I'm properly in New Orleans."

"I can take you to Pat O'Brien's for a Hurricane or three if you want the real deal."

She shook her head. "Touristy stuff isn't the real deal. Although I will *not* leave the city without first having some coffee and beignets at Café Du Monde, that's for sure."

"I've always admired your taste."

She leaned back against the counter and pointed her beer bottle at him. "Any sign of Sheen or her people?" In an ideal world, she'd be on hand when the fugitives made another move so she could capture them. A voice inside her noted that she'd shifted from killing terrorists to capturing fugitives when she thought of Sheen and her team, which was a change she had no problem with. It had always been her preference, really.

Chance shrugged. "Only at the Dragons, so far. We have someone there pretty much open to close keeping an eye out."

"Good plan. I still need to check it out for myself."

"We meet our contact there in an hour. Plenty of time to chat, maybe grab a snack while we wander over. You'll want to save your appetite for the house stew."

"Seriously?"

A quick grin leapt to his lips. "Seriously. Zeb makes great food and serves good drinks. There's a reason his place is so popular."

She changed the subject. "What do you know about the cult?"

"Let's have that conversation on the balcony." She followed him onto the shallow overlook above one of the Quarter's busy streets. It was only deep enough for a pair of chairs facing one another to rest in it sideways. They took them, and Tash grinned at the distant sound of a jazz band playing somewhere nearby.

Chance said, "So, aside from the information you provided, I haven't discovered much. I did confirm there have been a couple of incidents the rumor mill says involved a team of magicals going after a religious group. They figure it was two different religions duking it out, which is kind of funny to imagine. In this corner, the Pope. In that corner, the Buddha. Let's get ready to rumble!"

He laughed and continued, "The details fit well with the stuff you gave me. It's more or less common knowledge down here that the cult is present and active. No one pays much attention to it, though, no more than they do to rumors of voodoo activity."

She frowned. "That seems bizarre with people going missing."

He shrugged. "Not everyone is aware of the seriousness

of the situation, obviously. Overall, it adds to the city's mystique, which is likely what most locals care about. I've managed to secure a contact in the New Orleans Police Department who says the detectives are working the missing persons cases pretty hard but not coming up with anything yet. Seems like the zealots are good at covering their tracks."

She nodded. "Okay. That's a solid angle. Keep me in the loop. Now, I guess we should go meet your contact."

"You brought the cash?"

She patted the thigh pocket of her tactical pants. "I have it."

He grinned. "Then let's take a walk, shall we?" He tipped back his beer and finished it, and she did the same.

They meandered through the Quarter, heading for the edge where the Drunken Dragons tavern was. She followed Chance in, noting that he didn't let the door swing freely but opened it carefully and closed it gently behind them. Directly ahead was a three-sided bar, backed by a wall.

Behind it sat a dwarf with a wrinkled face that testified life experience and dark braided hair and beard streaked with a hint of gray. He nodded a neutral greeting at their entrance. Chance nodded back and touched her arm gently, tilting his head toward the main part of the room.

She followed him down the three steps to the main floor. It held three long tables running perpendicular to the bar, spottily filled with people drinking and eating, seated on benches and chairs across from one another. They passed through the space between the people closest to the street and the wall and made their way to the end of the table where a man sat. He was also eating and drinking, well-positioned to watch over the rest of the establishment.

They circled him and sat on the opposite side. In moments, a server appeared, took their orders for drinks and food, and vanished again, all in what seemed like a continuous blur of motion.

The man across the table didn't seem interested in talking. He kept all his attention focused on the act of devouring the stew and bread in front of him, and she didn't push the issue. His ears had the tiniest of curves at the top, suggesting elven blood somewhere in his background. His hair was dirty, and his clothes weren't much better.

He didn't register as homeless to her but did look like someone who spent a lot of his time partying and the rest of it recovering from partying in whatever location he happened to pass out. *Not sure this is a really reliable source in that case.*

Chance said, "Tash, this is Russel." The man finished his stew and pushed the bowl aside, then wiped his mouth with a napkin. When she finally met his gaze, she decided her initial assessment was off the mark. He was a professional, at least in the hours when he wasn't partying.

She asked, "Are you sure this is the best place to meet?"

He laughed. "Even if Zeb up there knows who you are, he also knows who I am. I'm a finder and fixer, which means I consort with people of every stripe. He won't pay it any mind if I'm talking to you. This is where the action is, so this is where I am, most of the time."

Chance asked, "What have you found out?"

He leaned forward and replied, "You've got what I asked for?"

Tash nodded. "I do. Answers first."

He shrugged. "Not a problem. I trust him. He trusts you, so we're good. You're looking for one Maîtresse Mambo Severine Eschete. She's the head honcho of all the deeply religious artifact wackos in town. Knowing about her is one thing but finding her is a whole different story. Lots of rumors."

He lowered his voice. "Including ones that talk about animated skeletons. And zombies. Not sure I would want to mess with her."

Tash considered that information for a moment. She replied, "It fits into the New Orleans theme pretty well. Maybe an exaggeration?"

Russel chuckled. "It does. When you think about it, someone under the influence of an artifact might be a zombie, in the science-fiction sense of the word rather than the undead one. Not in control of their actions. But probably not, you know, walking around moaning with their arms stretched out in front of them."

Chance added, "Unless it's Halloween or Mardi Gras. Then you'll find them on every corner." They all shared a laugh.

Tash said, "Time to start beating the bushes to locate this lady before our enemies do. At the same time, let's keep an eye out for them. Maybe the Mambo will be our lucky charm for catching Sheen or one of her people."

Zeb served his customers and bantered with Elena, his server, but never let his eyes drift too far from Russel and the other two in the corner. He was pretty sure he'd seen the man around from time to time, but that wasn't who interested him. The woman had never been in his bar before, but he recognized her from pictures Cara had shared as one of the people hunting them.

He waited until things slowed down a bit, growled, "Gotta go check the keg," and exited from behind the bar, taking the nearby staircase down to the basement. Once there, he pulled out the magical crystal that allowed him to communicate with Sheen's team. "Thought you should know that Natasha Kline is down here."

CHAPTER NINE

Bryant's steps were steady as he walked through the Washington, D.C. streets, his collar turned up against the unexpected light snow that had begun to fall. Someone seeing him wouldn't realize how much effort he put into keeping his stride stable.

The drug interactions he'd undergone to protect his team from Kevin Serrano had done some damage that hadn't yet cleared up. He was assured it would be soon and was on a regimen of drugs from science and magic potions to ensure that happened. However, he couldn't wait for a full recovery, not with something as important as what he thought was going on.

He'd taken the added measure of donning one of the team's illusion necklaces, which hadn't been in regular operation since their time setting up Two Worlds Security in Pittsburgh. It changed his face, seamlessly altering his features to those of someone who didn't resemble him at all. It would unfortunately set off magic detectors like Christmas Day carolers, so he couldn't use it to get into even moderate-security facilities. Still, it was quite sufficient for today's effort.

His clothes were Washington standard, a suit with a long dark wool overcoat buttoned up just high enough that his tie would still be visible, the ubiquitous mark of importance in town. He'd chosen power red for the outing, as his destination was one of the more conservative locations in the city.

Nestled between a coffee shop on one side and an Argentinian steak restaurant on the other, the aptly named Smoke had hardly any street frontage, only an ornate door with a sign above it. He pushed inside and let the outer door close before opening the inner one since the chill breeze also wanted access to the place. As soon as he stepped through the door, a woman in a business suit advanced to take his coat. He unbuttoned it to allow her to do so, and she handed him a metal chit in return.

He fished the golden key on its platinum ring from his pocket and held it up. A second woman, standing nearby, nodded. Had he not displayed the token, she would've escorted him into the modest main area reserved for the uninitiated. Instead, she took him through an unmarked door into the rear of the building, which the owner had divided into two sections, one small and one large. She left him alone in the first, a room paneled in dark, rich wood, with the same on both floor and ceiling. Three of the four walls held an extensive array of modest lockers of a somewhat lighter wood that worked perfectly in the space.

He opened the one that corresponded to his key and took out a cigar, leaving a shiny quarter coin behind in its place. He sauntered through the doorway into the main room, which held comfortable leather chairs, small tables, and female servers in rather tighter clothing than the ones outside had worn. The sweet smell of cigar smoke was everywhere, as was the ambiance of wealth.

It was a place Bryant wouldn't have chosen to patronize in most circumstances. However, his contact deep in the government power structure was a member, and this was the best way to reach her. When she next visited, which would almost certainly be within a few days, she would find the quarter in their shared locker and know he was looking for her.

He found a seat, allowed the elegant woman in the clingy red dress to clip and light his cigar for him, and nodded polite thanks. Leaning back in the chair, he drew on the Cohiba Esplendido while he waited for his drink order to arrive. *Sometimes the spy business has its small pleasures.*

It took almost forty-eight hours before he received the signal he wanted, days in which he meandered about the city seemingly at random. In reality, he spent the trips checking information drops that he'd once put in place. None of them would be used in his current operation, at least not as he envisioned it. Still, he had time to kill and a particular building to walk past on a regular basis, so doing a little preparatory work for later contingencies didn't hurt.

He wore a different face each time, the illusion necklace making that easy. His clothes were common enough to go unnoticed in the crowd. He passed a dozen people attired like him in any given hour.

Finally, the lamp in the apartment he routinely passed lit up, and the shade in front of it was half-drawn. That told him she'd received his signal and which method of communication his contact was using. He pulled out his phone and checked a message board for cigar aficionados, quickly spotting the entry that, in code, informed him where and when to meet. Both the lamp and the message were required. One without the other would alert him to a potential trap.

He killed time until evening with a nap in his hotel room and a decent dinner at a hole-in-the-wall Thai restaurant, then made his way to the movie theater. He wore his face now, but with subtle cosmetic touches to make it less likely he'd be recognized. His contact needed to see him since that was her defense against being trapped.

Bryant purchased his ticket and wandered into one of the several auditoriums within, taking a seat in the back. The place was fairly crowded, the weekly showing of classic science fiction films a draw for a quite heterogeneous bunch of people. After the lights went down and the movie started, a figure dropped into the chair next to his. He said, "Good pick."

The woman, a member of the House of Representatives and a fixture on various important committees, nodded. "Can't go wrong with David Lynch. Sand Worms. Ya hate 'em, right? I hate 'em myself."

He laughed at the mashup of *Dune* and *Beetlejuice*. "No question."

She remarked, "A call would've sufficed."

Bryant shook his head. "Guaranteed, your lines have taps." When she'd sat, he'd activated the jamming box that would take their phones and any other signals that might be coming from the nearby area offline.

She leaned closer so her words wouldn't carry. "Even so, now I'm some kind of conspirator, right?"

He chuckled. "You can say you were trying to get me to come in peacefully. Give up my team. Turn over a new leaf. You're powerful enough that no one will argue it."

"You're hot enough that they might. Your team's popping up all over the place. FBI, CIA, Homeland. Even the Army. Lots of ripples spreading through the government from the stones you're throwing."

"Seems out of proportion, doesn't it?"

She gave a small cluck in the back of her throat. "I was thinking the same thing."

Bryant drew a deep breath. He'd reached the moment of truth he'd been waiting for, but now that he stood on the precipice, he was worried about what he might find. *Still, we have to know. Knowledge is safety.* "I think we've touched on something bigger. Something involving artifacts, maybe. Or the vimana. Or the perspective of the government on magicals. Has anything changed, do you know?"

She sounded thoughtful. "That's a deep question. I'd say magicals are, in general, more accepted than you once were. But you know how the government is. Acceptance and usefulness are two sides of the same coin."

"So, what might those agencies you mentioned do to make magicals 'useful?'"

She chuckled low. "What *wouldn't* they do is probably

more the question. Before the current unpleasantness, your team was a model to be emulated."

"So, it's a big web, is what you're saying. Who's the spider at the center?" *There's always a spider at the center.*

"I don't know. I'm interested in finding out."

He nodded in approval of the notion. "What do you need from me?"

This time a laugh escaped her, loud enough to cause those nearby to turn and frown. She raised a hand in apology. "Oh, keep stirring the pot. We'll see what agitates to the top."

He smiled. "I can do that. I don't even need a reason."

She recognized the line and replied, "Watch out for gophers, Carl."

"You too." They watched the film in silence for a while. At the halfway mark, Bryant headed to the restroom and portaled away, back to the relative safety of Ruby's bunker. *Stirring the pot is something we're excellent at.*

CHAPTER TEN

Diana's relief was overwhelming when Bryant returned from D.C. She'd waited at the bunker for him, delaying her promised visit to Oriceran until she knew he was safe. She knew it wasn't rational, but since his kidnapping, the idea that he was in danger wouldn't leave her mind. Now, though, having greeted him and offered her goodbyes, she could finally get back to work.

Rath was on the other side of the bed where they'd laid out all of their gear. "Deep thoughts."

She nodded. "Yeah, a little. Worried about Bryant."

"He'll be fine. Max will protect him."

Diana shook her head. "That doesn't feel like enough. I have to ask you a big favor, buddy. I need you to stay here and look after him."

"Not go to Oriceran."

She sat on the bed with a sigh. "That's right. I know you wanted to go, and to be honest, I'd want you there as insurance in any other circumstance. Really, who knows what Nylotte has in mind?"

"Whatever it is, I'm sure it'll be fun."

"You have a strange definition of fun, Rath."

He stared at her, visibly upset, and she noted his purple hair looked particularly wild today. She sighed again. "Please do this for me. Watch over him whenever someone else isn't here to do it. I'm asking, not telling."

He nodded. "Will."

The knot in Diana's stomach loosened but didn't vanish. "All right. I guess I need to get geared up to do this thing." She'd already replaced the healing potion and energy potion capsules on her shoulders to ensure they'd be at maximum potency. She looked at the bulletproof vest, then set it aside with a sigh, knowing it wouldn't be useful against the sort of threats she'd face on the other planet. Technology worked unpredictably or not at all. Anyone foolish enough to fire a gun would most likely wind up with the weapon blowing up in their hand.

Even if they managed to shoot at her, she doubted that anti-magic ammunition had made it to Oriceran in any great quantity. So, she'd leave the vest and her pistols behind, along with her various technological or techno-magical gadgets.

She would take the modified comm, though, one of the first versions that employed both magic and technology. They hadn't tested it on the other planet, so this was as good a time as any to see if it would allow her to stay in contact. She didn't think the signal would have the power to cross from one world to the other, but the magical connections between them might be substantial enough that the system would work. *In any case, I won't depend on it.*

Rath asked, "Do you expect problems here?"

Diana shook her head. "No, but there's no way to be sure of it. Danger can pop up when you least expect it."

He laughed, and it sounded unforced, helping the knot in her stomach loosen a little more. "Danger is my middle name, baby." His Austin Powers accent was coming along. She rolled her eyes, then turned back to the task of gearing up. It was weird, going without the regular base layer and the standard uniform tunic. She pulled on her tactical pants and the boots with the blades hidden inside them. A Joan Jett concert t-shirt with a leather jacket over it finished the look.

Diana strapped Fury onto her back and slid on fingerless leather gloves to help her maintain her hold on its hilt. "I think I'm ready to go. Everything okay with you?"

He nodded. "Roger, Roger."

She countered, "All right, all right, all right," completing the cycle of quotes that annoyed their comrades. After wrapping him in a hug and whispering, "Thank you," she stepped through a portal to Oriceran.

It had been night on Earth, but it was late morning where she arrived on the magical planet. Her magic had delivered her to the familiar clearing in front of the cave Nylotte had located for them to use as a base. She turned in a confused circle, looking for the entrance.

Not finding it, she frowned and opened her magical senses. They revealed the nearby illusion concealing the cave's opening. She walked inside to find a small fire burning, the smoke escaping through a chimney carved into the stone.

Nylotte sat cross-legged before it, breaking sticks and throwing them into the flames. Occasionally she would pause in the destruction and immolation to put leaves into the pot suspended over the flames.

Diana sat across from her. "Have you been waiting here for me to show up?"

The Drow nodded. "I needed to spend some time in reflection and meditation, anyway. This was a good place to do it while I waited for your arrival." The white-haired warrior was in her battle garb, black leather armor that was more than it seemed, tooled with whirls and other designs that Diana always assumed were magical in some way. The hilts of dual swords stuck up over her shoulders, and she doubtless had more weapons hidden on her person.

Diana had given her a window, so it wasn't like she'd had to wait for days or anything. She gestured at the pot. "What are you making?"

"Replenishing tea."

She frowned. She couldn't recall her mentor ever needing to boost or refill her well of power. "What have you been up to?"

The Dark Elf shrugged. "A little of this, a little of that."

Diana realized her teacher wasn't in the mood to be forthcoming and knew better than to press. "Okay, then. What's the plan?

The Drow replied, "I've been spending some time wandering from place to place, collecting the gossip and news from various communities. I first got a hint that something unusual was going on a few months ago, and I've been pursuing it ever since. Turns out, it might have connections to your cult on Earth."

She frowned. "Really?"

Nylotte shrugged. "Emphasis on *might*. Whatever is going on involves artifacts, that's certain. I traveled to many of the places rumored to be home to Rhazdon's work and found others had recently visited several. I didn't go in. I wasn't willing to investigate any closer without support, not knowing what might await me."

"Well, support has arrived."

"Indeed, it has. That's one of the things we'll be doing."

"In addition to what?"

"We need to see if we can discover where this group—if it *is* a group—is working out of. For all we know, they've already collected dozens of artifacts and are a day away from launching whatever nefarious plan they're cooking up."

Diana frowned. "That's unlikely, though, right? They probably would've been noticed sooner if they'd been amassing that large an inventory of evil magic."

Nylotte threw the rest of the unbroken sticks she held onto the fire, then reached for the implements to strain the brew in the pot. "Or they've been doing it for a long time, very slowly. The point is, we have no way of telling what the situation is unless we take a walk and find out. So that's what we'll do."

"I'm in. My team and I owe you, after all."

The other woman nodded. "You do. Although, if we discover this connects to things on your planet, you'll owe me again."

Diana shook her head with a grin. "You're really something, you know?"

Nylotte finished pouring the liquid out of the cooking pot into two metal flasks, then slid them into holders on her belt. She poured the remainder into a mug that sat nearby, sipped, and grimaced. "Wicked stuff."

"I don't remember it tasting that bad."

The Drow chuckled. "You never got the full-strength version."

Diana decided she never wanted to try the undiluted brew. "I'm ready when you are."

Her mentor rose smoothly to her feet, dumped out the dregs of her cup, and waved to extinguish the fire magically. "Let's get a move on, then. Kyrstar is waiting for us near one of the locations where I thought I saw activity. Time to see if I was right."

CHAPTER ELEVEN

After their brief conversation, Diana and Nylotte portaled to a different location. She had no idea where on Oriceran they were, only that thick forest surrounded the small clearing they'd arrived in. It contained a structure that had probably been an imposing castle in the past.

Time had done its work, however, and the building would now do a poor job of holding off an encroaching army. It was made of weathered stone blocks, primarily gray but turning to white in places with dark swaths of dirt or prior damage decorating it in others. The outer wall had mostly crumbled, but it was possible to imagine from the pieces that remained where the main gate would've stood.

They strode through that opening and encountered a second protective barrier of stone and brick in better repair. It might've held off an invading army for up to five minutes before their attacks overcame the aged mortar that locked the blocks together. *Wonder if the place was attacked and fell into disrepair after, or if it simply fell apart.*

Off to the right, in between the two walls, sat Kyrstar. She leaned back against an upright section of the outer barrier and seemed unconcerned about anything. The Drow took a bite from the apple in her hand, chewed, swallowed, and finally deigned to acknowledge their presence. "About time you got here."

Diana scowled, but Nylotte only laughed. "Complaints, complaints. Always the same with you."

Kyrstar grinned and hopped up to her feet. The woman was younger than Nylotte, without the lines at the corners of her eyes that time or worry had given the other woman. Her hair was black and short, freely moving as she shifted position. On the whole, her figure looked more muscular than either Diana's or Nylotte's. She also wore black leather armor but nowhere near as fancy as Nylotte's.

On Kyrstar's left thigh was the sheath of a large dagger, almost a short sword, and on her right was a long pocket that encased three tubes, the outermost and the middle connected by a short chain visible where it stuck out of the holder. "So, are you finally ready to go see what's inside?"

Diana asked, "How long have you been watching?"

Kyrstar shrugged. "Several days, on and off. Solidly for the last eight hours, since your teacher there is excessively paranoid."

Nylotte replied calmly, with a hint of exasperation in her voice, "Keeping an eye on the place you're about to sneak into is simply a smart idea."

"You think all your ideas are smart."

"Because they are."

Diana shook her head and raised her hands. "Okay. You

two need to stop. I can't possibly cope with this nonsense. Let's get a move on."

The two Drow laughed—technically, the two *other* Drow since the Dark Elf legacy in her blood was the source of her magic powers—and they walked side-by-side into the next section of the castle's grounds.

The high doors guarding the structure itself were still present and were broad slabs of ancient wood. Thick metal bands ran across them at three-foot intervals to reinforce the tall barriers. Or, more accurately, they would've collectively been a barrier if one of the doors wasn't currently hanging off its hinges, half-detached. Diana asked, "What happened here?"

Nylotte shrugged. "Lost to history. We don't know."

"Then why do you think this is a relevant spot?"

Kyrstar replied, "There's a gnome settlement nearby. They've heard strange sounds coming from the area, animalistic, and in their words, 'terrifying.'"

She frowned. "Why haven't they investigated?"

"When the first of their group went missing, they sent a party to the castle. None of them returned. Since that time, they've focused on their defenses. Unfortunately, even with that precaution, several others have disappeared. All their best fighters were in the initial bunch they lost, so they're more or less out of options other than us."

Diana frowned again. It sounded too much like the cult's actions on Earth to be a coincidence. She asked Nylotte, "You think there's a Rhazdon artifact inside?"

Her teacher replied, "Historical rumors say there's one in this area or was at one time. Add in the missing people, and we've got a reasonable possibility that there's something to see inside. If not, or if it's not an artifact, we check off this one and move onto the next."

"Okay. I can see that."

Kyrstar said, "Nye, I think you're forgetting something." She lifted her hand and waggled it.

"You're right. Thanks for the reminder."

The interplay between the two Drow women was entirely unexpected. Diana's brain was having brutal convulsions, trying to align yet another version of her mentor with her beliefs about the woman. *Sarcastic teacher, wicked warrior, and now, a flirt? Nah. I'm sure misreading it.*

Nylotte reached into a pouch at her belt and extended an object to Diana. She accepted it and discovered a black leather cuff with metal charms woven into braided leather strips on its exterior.

She grinned. "New charms *and* a new bracelet? You're too generous."

Nylotte nodded. "I know. You're lucky to know me. You have a shield, you have a veil, you have an energy boost, and you have a decoy. You know the commands for the first three, and the command for the fourth is Lynshal."

Diana strapped on the cuff and mouthed the word, sending her magical energy into the charms to connect to them. After half a minute, she nodded. "Okay. I'm ready."

Kyrstar quipped, "I'm ready, too. Ready for a drink. At a bar. With more interesting company than you two."

"No one worth talking to is interested in conversing with you, except for us," Nylotte countered.

Kyrstar laughed happily. "It's your monosyllabic vocabulary. I can't get enough of it. Drives me wild."

As they crossed the threshold and entered the castle,

Nylotte ordered, "Focus. Weapons." She drew her paired swords, holding them like knives, the right one reversed along her forearm, the other point down low in front of her.

It was a style Diana hadn't seen before with weapons that large. *Guess I need to make more time for training.* She drew Fury and felt the connection as the sentient being inside it acknowledged her presence and matched his will to hers.

Kyrstar pulled the strange set of rods from her thigh sheath. Once extracted, it revealed three sections connected by chains. In this configuration, she would probably use the pieces in her left and right hands as bludgeoning sticks and the middle for blocking.

Diana had seen similar weapons in martial arts movies but hadn't the first idea of how to use one effectively. *Nylotte said she's a skilled healer. Maybe she tries to be less damaging.*

The other woman put that notion to rest as she deftly brought the pieces into line, *clicked* them together, and twisted. Sharp spear points extended from each side of the weapon, now a long staff. She twirled it around several times, finishing with it in guard position across her body.

A strange sensation tickled Diana's brain as she realized she was likely the least skilled of the three. *That* was a situation she hadn't faced in some time. She didn't ruminate on the idea, simply followed her mentor and the other Drow into the castle.

The entryway rose to three stories, with staircases leading up out of it. The design was defensive since they provided the only way to leave the room. Murder holes at every other step indicated the presence of a passage between the castle's inner and outer walls.

Diana shook her head. "They were pretty serious about defending this place."

Nylotte nodded. "Standard tactics. Especially when you're fighting magic. Exposing as little of yourself as possible tends to be a good idea. So, watch for traps."

Kyrstar muttered, "New ones, or old ones?"

"Both. And both physical and magical. If people are using this as a base, it would be foolish of them not to leave some tricks in the path of an unwanted visitor."

"Well, that's antisocial. One more reason not to like them," Diana quipped.

Nylotte led them to the right-hand staircase, and they carefully ascended it. Kyrstar, in the lead, abruptly stopped a third of the way up and snapped her staff to horizontal so they couldn't pass her. "Pressure plate on the next step."

Nylotte whispered an incantation. "I don't sense any magical traps nearby."

"In that case, we should be good to step over it. Still, let me check." Kyrstar extended the staff and poked the stair above that one to no effect. The same happened with the next, but the third, which would've been a difficult reach for someone lacking a long weapon, activated when she touched it.

Spikes shot up from below, breaking through the thin veneer of stone that had concealed them. Anyone stepping on it would likely have had their foot destroyed by the spikes, which were needle-sharp and placed tightly together, like the bristles on a brush.

Nylotte sighed. "It's tiresome being right all the time."

Kyrstar frowned. "We'll keep testing every step. You look out for magical stuff. I'll focus on the physical. Earth girl, watch our backs."

Diana sighed at the snarky comment but let it pass unanswered. The staircase yielded a second trap, a thin stiff wire that jutted out from the side. They maneuvered around it, and the staff triggered the trap that lay beyond, another set of the spikes to catch those who thought they'd evaded the danger.

"Two in a row," Nylotte remarked.

Kyrstar nodded. "Which means the third will be markedly different." Finally, they reached the second level. It was a single platform with only one corridor leading from it. Their point person asked, "Go up to three instead?"

Nylotte shook her head. "The castle is in disrepair. The upper floors are likely at least partially open to the elements. No one would make their base up there."

Kyrstar grumbled, "So, the corridor that's a funnel for invaders, it is." The other Drow paused while Nylotte cast spells at the landing inside the staircases on their level.

Nylotte explained, "Alarms. In case anyone tries to get in behind us."

Kyrstar snorted. "Because they'll certainly use the stairs."

"Shut it."

Diana stifled a laugh. *Guess picking up habits goes in both directions.*

They entered the corridor and made it halfway down the dark passage before a corner appeared ahead. They navigated it carefully and discovered a switchback that took them almost the same distance back toward the front of the castle. There, they found another corner, followed by another switchback.

Diana muttered, "Okay, when I said they were serious about defense, I understated the matter."

Kyrstar replied, "Let's hope the ones who cared enough to create all this stuff were the original inhabitants, not the current ones." The pit that opened under her feet as she took her next step suggested their collective concerns were well-founded.

CHAPTER TWELVE

Kyrstar immediately bounced back out of the pit, able to do so because Nylotte had reacted quickly and jammed her sword in the mechanism before the doors could close over their partner. The Drow healer grumbled, "Scumbags."

Nylotte observed, "Clever, requiring a certain weight to trigger it."

Which explains why it didn't go off when she poked it with her staff.

Words echoed through the chamber as if hidden speakers surrounded them. "Come ahead, magic wielders, and embrace your fate." The voice was male, deep and resonant as it bounced off the walls, but also slightly raspy.

Diana asked, "Is it me, or does that *not* sound like something a sane person would say?"

Nylotte laughed. "As if you're an expert on sanity, my student."

Kyrstar made a *shushing* noise. "They obviously know we're here. Let's get this done before they come up with something else clever to throw in our path." She snapped force blasts at the floor as they advanced, triggering another pit along the way, as well as a particularly wicked trap that shot darts from the walls, floors, and ceiling across a three-foot section of the corridor.

Finally, they emerged into a room that had likely been a reception hall in the castle's original days. Now, it was the living space of many beings, definitely more than should've called it home.

The first thing Diana's senses registered as they stepped inside was the incredibly foul stench. The second was that the chamber was huge, probably the whole back half of the castle long, encompassing the inner three-quarters of the width.

Chandeliers hung in a line from the entranceway to a large seat in the center, above a tattered carpet that looked like it might've once been ornate. The ancient throne of stone and wood at the end of it supported a single lounging figure, seeming almost as if it had fallen there and never bothered to wriggle into the seat properly.

Apart from that lighted strip in the center, the chamber was dark. She sensed movement along the outer sections and heard noises coming from them, low growls, *hisses*, and whispers. She gripped Fury tighter, had a moment of wishing Rath was there and being thankful he wasn't, and followed the other Drow women. They seemed unconcerned with the beings to their left and right, focused instead on the man waiting on the throne before them.

He called, "Wait, my children. Let's see what these trespassers have to say for themselves before we eat them." Answering snarls sounded from all directions.

Nylotte drawled, "Well, that explains the smell."

The man sat up and leaned forward toward them. His hair was a long, matted mass, pulled away from his face and bound with a leather cord at the top of his head. His tattered clothes consisted of nothing more than a robe that might've come from the castle's initial occupants, to judge by its decayed state. He held no weapons, and his feet were bare. He demanded, "Why are you here?"

Kyrstar replied, "To help you. I'm a healer. I can remedy whatever ails you."

He cackled loudly. "Why, *nothing* ails us, stranger, save a lack of gnome flesh for feasting. You haven't brought us some, have you?" The question was a taunt, and the unseen people around them laughed.

Nylotte let out a weary sigh. "It doesn't have to be this way. We can help your people, something a good leader would certainly desire."

He stood angrily and pointed at her. "I say to you, again, we need no help."

Diana turned at the sound of movement behind her and saw another man, similar in looks and attire to the first, step into the light a dozen feet away.

Nylotte replied, "Unfortunate. Then, I guess, embrace your fate."

———

Nylotte blasted through the air on a burst of force magic, flying over Kyrstar and landing in front of the man they'd been speaking to. She and the Drow healer had fought before often enough that their moves were intuitive. While

Nylotte addressed the main threat, her partner would deal with whatever else presented itself, in this case, the unseen people around them. She whipped her right-hand sword forward in a high slash, trying to end the fight with a single decapitating blow.

His laughter rang out at the start of her move. By the time it was halfway through, purple tendrils of shadow magic had exploded from his arms, reaching out to snare each of her wrists. *Two artifacts. No wonder he's insane.*

In her awareness, only artifacts designed to work together, through some arcane pairing only Rhazdon understood, could do so without dire consequences for their host. Since Rhazdon's Vengeance and Rhazdon's Defense remained lost, this was *not* an example of one of those sanity-preserving arrangements.

Her swords were both artifact weapons. She yanked her arms together, using the blade in the opposite hand to cut through the magical tendrils securing her wrists. That she was able to do so was a measure of his relative weakness in overall magical and physical strength, despite the power of his artifacts.

Nylotte snapped her foot up in a front kick, and it met a force barrier. She slashed down with both swords, aiming for his legs, but the man launched himself up and back to avoid it. She pointed her right-hand sword and willed magic through it, and a line of force reached out to snag his foot.

A yank of the sword compromised his flight path, dropping him hard on the back of the throne. He clattered off the stone seat and landed with a groan on the floor beside it. Nylotte stomped forward to deliver the death blow and remove his evil from the universe.

Diana raced at the one behind them as soon as Nylotte made her move. Shadow tendrils lashed out from his left arm, seeking to grab her throat, but she sliced Fury through them in a downward chop, then circled the blade for a stroke at the top of the arm itself, hoping to eliminate the artifact's threat by removing the limb. Her sword met a shadow blade that materialized in the other figure's hand. The magical weapon slapped hers aside and shifted into a guard position.

She met her opponent's gaze. Unlike the figure on the throne, this one still retained at least some sanity. His lips twisted in a sour grin, and malevolence radiated from him as he slid sideways, stalking in a circle toward her weak side. She moved with him, cognizant of the potential danger behind her from whoever made the sounds coming from the room's perimeter but focused on the immediate threat.

His blade stabbed at her throat. She slipped aside to avoid it, then stepped forward and slammed a hammer fist strike into his solar plexus with her left hand. The blow took him by surprise, aided by her movements sped up by threading magic to her muscles, and he staggered backward.

She tried the same attack again, but he brought his arm down to block, so she cut at his torso on the opposite side.

Tentacles reached out to grab Fury and wrestled with her for possession of the blade.

She leapt up, spinning and twisting to use her move's momentum to break its hold. She hit the floor, rolled, and surged to her feet, meeting the descending shadow blade with Fury. The magic weapon slid down to the pommel before stopping. She snapped out a kick that drove the other figure back, then had to scurry to the side as figures appeared out of the dark.

Kyrstar ran for the darkened wall of the room, which became notably less dark as her natural lowlight vision compensated. The area was full of people. Each appeared to be in a far worse state than the man on the throne.

Despite their weakness, they shuffled steadily toward her. Long, sharp fingernails reached out with hunger, anger, and desperation on their faces. *Mostly hunger, whether for violence or my flesh, I don't know. Not that it matters. They can't have the one, and they're about to get more of the other than they could desire.*

She set her jaw, resigning herself to the need to hurt people she might rather have helped in a different situation. Then she swirled through them, using her staff to keep them at a distance, changing directions and strike angles each time the weapon halted from impacts on muscle and bone. She stabbed and smashed, moving toward the back of the room, figuring Nylotte would be smart enough to retreat if a substantial number came to the aid of the figure she fought.

After a dozen were down, the press got too thick for her to wield the long weapon, so she twisted it the right way to transform it from spear into a three-section staff. The wicked tips stayed, and now she struck at closer range, stabbing with the left and right and positioning the middle section to prevent attacks from landing on her torso. She blocked kicks and grabs from below with effective stomps of her feet, her mind and body fully committed to self-defense and clearing the foes surrounding her.

She found a moment to breathe after stabbing both sharpened points into the chest of a woman trying to claw at her throat and saw that both Diana and Nylotte were still fighting. An instant later, the moment of relative peace was over. She dashed at the next opponent, leapt, and delivered a front kick to the face that knocked him into the arms of those nearest. They threw him aside and came at her in a wave, screaming with rage and anger.

Diana felt the hands of an enemy lash her back as she blocked a strike from the artifact wielder before her and snapped, "Lynshal." A flash of light burst from her wrist, and she dashed to the side. When the brilliance faded, six of her were present in the immediate area, five of them identical magical copies. They ran in random directions, waving copies of Fury. That occupied the newcomers for a moment, and she used the time to deal with the one in front of her.

He'd been stunned by the burst of illumination but recovered quickly, sending tentacles stabbing at her again.

She sliced from inside out with Fury, chopping them off, then reversed the path to cut into them closer to the artifact. He threw a punch with his other arm, and she raised her left to block but otherwise ignored it.

Fury swiped across again, cutting the tentacles back more. Her next cut, angled to counteract the fact that he was yanking the arm away, slashed through the limb at the elbow. He collapsed as if the artifact had been the only thing keeping him up, and the magical item crawled toward her.

She summoned a force cube around it, making sure to slide a thin film of the magic underneath so it couldn't somehow dig out, then turned to deal with the rabble that had emerged from the edges.

By the time Nylotte had reached the fallen man, he was up again. They'd traded blows, her sword slicing his tentacles, while he managed to sneak a couple of them by her defenses to strike her in painful but not vital spots. Her muscles would ache more than usual after this fight, given the bludgeoning they were taking. She spun a web of shadow tentacles at his feet, hoping to halt his frenetic movements, but he hopped over the attack and kept circling the throne.

He effectively kept the large chair interposed between them as a barrier to prevent her strongest sword attacks, leaving her to trade magical bursts with him while trying to defend against the artifacts. It wasn't a sustainable situation, as indicated by the sound of scuffling from the surrounding area, which informed her that time was of the essence. She whispered the command to activate a shield from her charm bracelet and charged in, trusting its strength to protect her from the artifact's tentacles.

They scraped against the oval barrier but failed to penetrate. She sent a surge of power through her body to increase her speed, reached him, stepped forward, and drove her left-hand sword through her shield and into his throat. He looked stunned, his eyes wide and his mouth gaping, then collapsed in a heap. The two artifacts burst from his flesh and scampered in different directions. She levitated them where they could do no harm, then set herself to deal with the encroaching enemies.

It took less than a minute to finish the remainder, all of whom continued attacking even when offered a truce. As they gathered together afterward, Kyrstar produced three ornate boxes from her backpack, and Nylotte used her magic to lower the artifacts into them. Diana asked her, "Do you want me to take these back to Earth?"

Nylotte shook her head. "I have a place for them in the city where I was born. No one would think to look for them there."

Her student grinned. "A Drow city? Can I come?"

She chuckled. "Not now, but perhaps later. Return to your planet, rest, do what you have to do. We'll call for you when we have the next potential location."

CHAPTER THIRTEEN

Sloan had hoped that the woman, Lila, would've chosen to escort him to the "Meeting of like-minded people." Unfortunately, when he'd texted her, she'd simply replied with the time and a place. The former was eight p.m., and the latter was the church that Rath's contacts on the Network—*the Trollnet, heh*—had identified. He'd dressed up for the occasion, well, dressed up by Chuck's standards, anyway. An off-the-rack suit, middle-quality dress shirt, and a pedestrian brown tie. *Really killing it, Chuck.*

Once in a while, Sloan took a vacation and put on the personality of a swanky person used to the best in life. He spent a couple of days in that skin getting pampered by well-paid hotel and spa staff. *I could use one of those right about now. But no, I'm headed for a meeting with what's probably a murderous cult. Hi, I'm Chuck. What do you do? Oh, human sacrifice? How interesting. Tell me more.*

He snorted as he exited the autonomous vehicle and made his way up the hill to the church. It was called the

Church of the Avenged Angel and looked entirely legitimate from the outside. Spotlights highlighted the greenery, and more of them illuminated the grandiose gothic structure, which featured many points and levels climbing to the sky. The huge double doors that were doubtless the main sanctuary entrance stood closed, but a lit path led to a side door. He walked up a short flight of stairs and entered.

The entryway was warm, with a coat rack on the right that he hung his overcoat on. A bulletin board nearby held messages from one congregant to another, as well as the theme of the Sunday sermon, which was "Justice for all." He kept his face neutral, but inside, he snarked, *A little on the nose, don't you think?*

Noises came from down a hallway, and he headed in that direction, eventually entering into a big social room, the same kind as every church he'd ever been inside. A table on the right held urns of coffee, cans of soda, and boxes of homemade cookies. He declined to partake since they might have magical or chemical enhancements, and Chuck would have no way to detect that.

He spotted Lila across the room and gave her a little wave, which she acknowledged with a nod. Her attention was all for the man who stood next to her. *Although she probably thinks of it as her standing beside him, that being the order of the relationship.*

The man was tall, halfway between six and seven feet. He, too, wore a suit, the only other person present doing so. The fit bespoke custom tailoring and the accessories and dress shirt were far higher quality than Chuck's. He was sandy-haired, healthy in that California money way, and had seemingly flawless skin and no facial hair.

Sloan people-watched as more folks drifted in to join the dozen or so that were there when he arrived. By the time the clock struck eight, the group had taken most of the folding seats. He remained standing in the back, leaning against the far wall opposite the small stage and podium that occupied one side of the room.

The man bounded up a couple of stairs to it, grabbed the microphone attached to a stand at the podium, and walked away so nothing would separate him and his audience. *Public speaking skills. Check.*

His voice was deep and melodious, with an edge of good humor, as if life was a joke and they were all in on it together. Lila also climbed onto the small stage but stayed in the wings, seeming for all the world like an assistant. *Or maybe an acolyte? Subordinate, in any case.* "Our theme on Sunday will be justice. Not coincidentally, our subject tonight is justice, as well."

The crowd nodded, and a smattering of applause sounded. He continued speaking on the topic, and Sloan moved a little to the side to better see the audience's reactions. The strong majority already looked convinced and had entered as true believers. A couple of women and one other man he'd seen talking to Lila seemed less enthusiastic at his words, perhaps listening with the desire to be persuaded but not quite arriving at that destination yet. *Good setup, putting your targets in an alleged peer group that's mostly filled with plants who already support you.*

Once he got rolling, the man on the stage was a dynamo, his calm demeanor replaced by quick movements, variations in tone and speed, and suffusive energy. The smile never left his face, no matter the seriousness of the topic, and the edge in his tone that seemed amused persisted, as well.

He asked, "So what can we do when certain groups are treated differently than others? Those with different skin color, those with different gender, those who might be from a different country?" He paused to let the moment hang, then added, "Or a different planet?"

His voice fell like he was confiding something. "Or those who might have ancestors from that other planet?"

The whole crowd nodded, including the ones Sloan had identified as newcomers. The speaker discussed the plight of magicals, how mundanes often discriminated against them, and how it was the responsibility of everyone, magical or not, to stop such things.

He explained, "That's one of the things we do right here, in my church. We bring magicals and non-magicals together in a spirit of community. We don't care what deity you worship, as such. Of course, we have our beliefs and will share them with anyone who wishes to listen, but our overriding mission is peace. That means bringing people together in support of one another."

Sloan had listened to con artists and confidence men aplenty during his career and had used the same linguistic and delivery tricks innumerable times in his operations. The man came across like a believer, but something about him didn't quite fit that persona. Sloan concentrated, trying to summon his flash, not that it worked like that, and was rewarded only with failure. The speaker finished with some closing remarks and stepped down from the stage to greet the people in the audience.

Sloan continued to watch, noting how Lila stayed at his side, deflecting some folks while encouraging others into his presence. The man made a special effort to interact with the ones Sloan had identified as new. Finally, when most everyone had moved to the doors or the food and drink table, he walked over to Sloan and stuck out a hand.

"Kenneth Lytle. Lila has told me how you two met. Says you seem like a pensive sort and took forever to approach her in the bar."

He laughed. "Oh, she did, did she?" He released the other man's hand. "I'm Chuck Waserman. It's not like I was stalking her or anything. She's kind of impossible not to notice."

The other man lifted a well-manicured eyebrow. "Perhaps it was she who was stalking you."

Sloan shook his head. "If so, she was remarkably subtle about it. Especially by talking to all those other people and never once saying a word to me."

Lila replied, "Perhaps my methods are simply inscrutable."

He laughed. "Indeed, they are that."

The other man asked, "So what did you think? You are, of course, welcome to join us for our services on Sunday as well."

Sloan shook his head. "I'm not much of a worship service sort of person, thanks. I do agree with a lot of what you said. Community is important, and treating everyone as equals within it, vital."

Kenneth gave him a considering look. Then he

ventured, "Wouldn't you agree we need people who can lead, and that in turn means others have to follow?"

Sloan shrugged. Chuck would have no idea what was coming, even though he was pretty sure he did. "Agreed."

"So, equality is never perfectly equal."

He tilted his head slightly to the side. "Are you going all Orwell on me now?"

Kenneth clapped. "Two legs good, my friend. No, not Orwell. I will say that most of the people in this room tonight don't have the capacity to lead. They can be good workers, evangelists, helpers, and caretakers. But *not* leaders.

"What we're really searching for is the sort of person who can accept that mantle of responsibility and do the hard things that need doing. That's what Lila looks for. That's what she tells me she sees in you." The tall man stepped back, clearly disengaging. "So, I hope we'll see you back here sometime soon, maybe talk a little further about it."

Sloan blinked at the sudden disconnect, then stumbled over his words. "Sure. Cool. Until then, I guess."

Lila smiled at him and followed her boss. Sloan lingered for a few minutes, waiting to see if anything else would occur, but nothing did. He gave a mental sigh and headed for the exit, thinking that reeling in this particular fish was taking much too long. *Dynamite fishing, that's where it's at. Maybe I need to talk to Anik.*

It came as a surprise when Lila showed up at his side in the parking lot. She asked, "How about a drink?"

He grinned. "Love one."

They used a portal to get from the church to the street

outside The Mill. They went inside, and he followed her to her regular table and took the seat across from her. Drinks appeared in the hands of a server, the usual for both of them, with a wave from the wizard behind the bar. She said, "Kenneth was impressed with you."

Sloan chuckled. "I don't think so. Seemed like a standard speech, all of it. Very well-rehearsed."

She shrugged and leaned back. "The one doesn't preclude the other. Yes, he's a church leader. Minister, if we're being formal about it. Of course, he's got the patter down."

"The message and the delivery both were extremely on point. Seems like your group has its head on straight."

She nodded. "I agree. And I think you can help. Interested in joining us?"

"In what capacity?"

"Outer inner circle. People who are trusted, but not all the way inside. That level takes time and experience."

He laughed. "Now it's sounding like a pyramid scheme again."

She grinned. "Only one way to find out. Join us. I promise you won't regret it." Something in her tone suggested fringe benefits might be on the table. *Giving me what I want and the potential of a bonus as well? How could I resist?*

"I don't see any downsides here. I'm in."

CHAPTER FOURTEEN

Rath wasn't pleased with Diana's last-minute decision to leave him behind during her trip to Oriceran. He'd watched enough *Dr. Phil* on TV to have some insight into how people thought, and his armchair psychologist concluded that almost losing Bryant had scared Diana. Now she was overreacting to protect *him*.

As if I need protecting. She's the one who needs protecting. He'd wanted to argue but had seen that she wouldn't listen because she was too worried, so he'd put on a happy face and agreed.

Nevertheless, he wasn't a happy troll. *More like a frustrated one.* His success in getting the Trollnet operational had been a recent high point, and so was reconnecting with Professor Charlotte and Manny. Aside from that, things of late had landed more in the negative bucket than the positive one.

However, since he was a *smart* troll, he knew the solution. He had to do something he loved to break the moodiness, something that would make him happy and permit no hint of negativity. So, he stood atop the Cathedral of Learning in Pittsburgh in the early evening, with his flight suit wrapped around him and the air currents highlighted in his goggles. He ran the few steps to the edge and leapt into the air with a shout, then slapped the button to extend the wings.

Kayleigh had found time to upgrade the suit slightly. She'd set up a connection between his goggles and the wings that allowed Gwen to activate them if something happened to him, like he suddenly passed out the moment he soared off a building. Not that it was ever likely to happen. *I guess Kayleigh is concerned about everyone's safety, too.*

He shook his head as he banked toward a nearby updraft. *Everyone's a little on edge. Difficult times. We'll come through it. That's what families do. We just have to give each other what we need. And I have a need. A need for speed.*

While he'd far prefer to be with Diana on Oriceran, being able to soar through the skies of the town he loved was an excellent consolation prize. He banked toward the neighborhood that held Manny's and Charlotte's house, making a pass over its roof. A light was on in the window, and he thought he'd glimpsed one or both as he passed. The streets around the home were serene, absolutely no sign of danger, and a checkmark went in a little mental box for his old friends. *Heh. They wouldn't like me calling them old, even though that's not how I meant it.* "Gwen, let's check out the graveyard."

A new vector appeared in his goggles, and he shifted his direction to align with it. The lack of communication from Amadeo was another ongoing source of frustration. He kept the cell phone on him at all times, making sure it was powered up and ready to receive, but so far, it had remained inert. Every time he left a signal-blocking location, like Ruby's bunker, he checked it hopefully. Still, nothing.

He descended into a landing, slapping the button to retract the wings and hitting the ground at a run to absorb his momentum. His goggles flickered through detection modes. No heat signatures larger than small animals were present. A sigh escaped him as he wandered through the headstones, which were a mix of old and new-ish, some from as far back as almost three centuries.

He approached the mausoleum and stopped five feet away from the short flight of stairs that led up to the door and the grate that protected it. He had faith that eventually Amadeo would reach out to him and slightly less faith that he could convince the assassin to help him. He wouldn't stop hoping and trying until he knew one way or the other.

After ten minutes of letting his mind wander and his gaze travel over the rest of the graveyard and the starry sky above, Rath shook himself out of his contemplation. He climbed the fence to get out of the cemetery and made his way to the nearest high building, a seven-story parking garage a few blocks away.

He walked around the upper level, looking for an air current that would provide some lift, and found one that looked viable. It would be a leap of faith, of a sort, but one without too much downside. If the airflow failed to deliver the buoyancy he required, he'd simply land on the ground and look for a new option.

He'd walk back to the cathedral and launch from there

again if he had to. Flying was his happy place, and he had several hours before Ruby would open a portal back to her bunker so he could wait for Diana to return. He leapt, extended his wings, and got the updraft he needed. He moved from that one to another and realized he'd unconsciously chosen a useful direction. "Gwen, plot path to Chan."

"Will do," the AI replied, and an orange line appeared in his display. He'd abandoned the gamified interface with its triangles and sound effects for the evening, preferring the purity of his normal flight. He was surprised to see an outside light on when he neared the building Chan used as a home and training space. With a surge of hope, he landed in front of the door and knocked. A grin spread across his face as a familiar voice said, "Please come in, Rath."

He walked inside. The place hadn't changed since his prior visits. It was still largely set up as a training area, with mats on the floor and targeting dummies on the far end. Chan's were specially outfitted with visual and sonic targets because the blade master who'd taught Rath how to throw knives was blind.

Chan sat along the wall on the opposite side of the room from the mannequins, smiling in Rath's direction. He looked a little older than Rath remembered, but not all that much. His thin form hid a wealth of martial talent.

Rath approached him and gave a bow appropriate from student to teacher, and the man returned it with a nod. When he spoke, his voice was full of warmth. "How have you been, my friend?"

Another stool rested beside Chan, and Rath jumped

onto it and sat. "Good. Some challenges. Everyone healthy and safe. You?"

"The same. This old body creaks a bit more with each new day, but that's normal and natural and not to be worried about. Or so my doctor tells me." They laughed together, and Chan continued, "I'm glad you chose to stop by today."

"Checked last time I was in the city, but everything was dark." He frowned as a thought struck him. "Why was light on tonight?"

Chad laughed. "Now that you're back in town sometimes, everyone is keeping an eye out for you. Well, 'everyone' is Charlotte and Manny, but anyway, they have cameras watching in all directions from their house. They spotted you flying overhead and let me know. I must say, I'm a little offended at not being invited to be a part of your communication network." His grin showed that he was teasing.

Rath laughed. "Happy for you to join Trollnet. I'll bring you a device next time."

Chan nodded. "So, are your skills as good as they were? Or, hopefully, better?"

"Still training. Still improving."

"Prove it." He gestured at the targets on the other side of the room. Rath hopped enthusiastically off the stool and slipped out of his flying harness. When he was ready, he drew a deep breath to steady himself. Chan interrupted. "Blindfolded." His outstretched hand offered a wrap of cloth.

Rath giggled. "Same old Chan."

The blind man laughed. "When you reach my age, not much changes."

"So you say. Perhaps you need more adventures."

The man smiled. "Perhaps, my friend."

Unlike so many people who used the phrase "My friend," his blade instructor gave the impression that he meant it, that their connection was as strong as it had ever been, and that it would endure through all things. Rath aspired to be that sort of person and counted himself lucky to be surrounded by others who shared that trait.

He finished wrapping the strip around his head and focused on the soft sounds emanating from the targets. Each was slightly different, an alteration in pitch or volume that allowed him to separate them. "Ready."

"Begin."

Rath cross-drew two knives and threw them both over-hand, aiming at the leftmost targets. Before they struck, he already had the next pair in his hands, and they were flying toward the center targets as the first two landed with a satisfying simultaneous *thunk*. The last pair were on their way before the middle ones hit their marks. A moment later, he'd successfully put a blade into each of the target dummies.

From behind him, Chan observed, "Well done. Six for six. Your skills haven't slipped."

"I had the best teacher."

Chan laughed. "Oh, I don't know about that. Now, retrieve your knives and join me for some tea."

Rath removed the blindfold and did as instructed, following the man into his small living quarters in the back corner of the room. The kitchen was cozy, with a small table and four chairs taking up most of its space.

Chan had already set out a teapot. He prepared water in an electric kettle, sharing the details of his life since they'd last seen each other. He put tea in the pot and filled it, then poured when it was ready. They sipped their brew and ate a few cookies out of a plastic package. When Chan finished speaking, Rath took his turn and shared his adventures, generating surprise and laughter in equal measure.

When he stopped, Chan shook his head. "That's an impressive life you're living. It seems to suit you."

Rath nodded. "It does."

"It includes a lot of danger, does it not?"

He shrugged. "Diana has a job to do. I'm her partner." Really, there was nothing more to say.

"With that in mind, I have a present for you." Chan rose and left the room, heading into a portion of his living area Rath had never visited. He returned a moment later with a wooden case. He set it on the table and opened it to reveal six shining throwing knives. Rune work covered each with arcane symbols etched over the entire surface. Five of them were identical, the sixth different.

Rath breathed, "They're beautiful."

Chan nodded. "The person who filled this commission is a master of the art. I ordered these long ago and am happy they have finally reached your hands, for which I intended them."

Rath picked one up and held it, admiring the balance. "Are the etchings only decorative?"

Chan shook his head with a smile. "Good insight, my friend. No. These weapons will hold magic and discharge it upon impact. The five that are similar will contain magical lightning. You can have one of your friends charge it with a spell at a level that will stun, or a level that will do more."

He grinned. It was a perfect gift and would certainly prove useful in the days to come. "And the sixth?"

"That one is less versatile. It holds fire. The likelihood of someone struck with that weapon surviving is rather low."

"For emergencies, then."

"That was my thought."

"May I switch them with my others and leave those with you?"

Chan smiled. "Of course."

Rath slotted them into the sheaths in his vest, exchanging them with his usual knives. The deadly one went in as if it was heavier than the others, even though he knew it wasn't. "I have to go, unfortunately. Could I maybe come back for a lesson sometime soon?"

Chan laughed. "Of course. You owe me a communication device, anyway."

Rath grinned. "Definitely. Must have you on the Trollnet."

CHAPTER FIFTEEN

Rath left Chan's house in high spirits with a broad smile. No tall buildings lay nearby, unfortunately, so he had to walk a few blocks to the nearest launch point. His time in Pittsburgh extended for a couple more hours, and even if he didn't fly anymore tonight, it had been an unqualified success on all levels. *Sometimes, things work out.*

The phone in his belt pouch vibrated. Rath withdrew it and opened it to see a picture of the city's baseball stadium. It was from Amadeo, and he could only assume the man wanted him to go to the ballpark.

It was a good walk, about a half-hour at his current size. Still, the cold didn't bother him, especially in his flight suit, and he didn't have much to worry about from anyone who might come across him. Generally, people reacted well to him. Those who didn't tended to run when he showed him his eight-foot size. *Not to mention the knives.*

He walked on, admiring the stars he could see despite the city lights that competed with them and exchanging smiles with the few pedestrians he encountered. The path between his current position and the thriving district around the sports stadiums was mostly undeveloped land, some businesses, some industrial storage, but nothing exciting.

When he was about two blocks away from his destination, the phone *buzzed* again. He'd been carrying it open the whole time and looked down to see a picture of a statue. He recognized the monument honoring Roberto Clemente, a famous baseball player who had once played for the home team. He switched directions at the next block, heading up to the statue's area rather than toward the nearest access to the park.

When he arrived, the phone *buzzed* again. It had a picture of the Pirates' dugout. *Okay, guess I'm supposed to get inside.* The closest entrance was locked, and he assumed the rest would be as well, but that wasn't a problem for him.

The building's façade was brick, large blocks with enough of a groove between them that he could wedge his fingers into them. He climbed up about a story, then found his ascent blocked by a flat expanse. He checked left and right, but no other path offered itself. Again, though, it was a challenge he could easily overcome.

He fired his grapnel upward, and it stabbed into a wooden sign on the top ridge of the stadium. He pulled himself up to the next climbing location and eventually made it to the top. He retrieved his grapnel and rewound the line, resetting his launcher in case he needed it again.

The facility wasn't in use during the winter since the football and hockey teams had their stadium and arena, respectively. He traveled down through vacant seats and hopped over the barriers between sections until he arrived at the field. He walked out to the pitcher's mound and stood there for a moment, looking around at the stands and turning to see the outfield wall with the city sparkling behind it. With a smile, he made his way toward the dugout.

A door leading from the covered space into a hallway was open, so he shoved the phone in his pocket and walked in that direction. Because it was Amadeo, he kept a wary eye out for traps in the corridor but saw none. The tunnel turned and eventually opened into a large locker room. As he stepped inside, a voice ordered, "Set the knives down, and put the batons beside them."

Rath complied, added his goggles to the pile, and took several steps away from them without being asked since he knew the assassin would prefer it. A green light appeared with a *snap* as Amadeo broke a glow stick and threw it on the floor between them. The man wore his usual all-black uniform, very similar to the ones the agents used. He only had a half-mask on today, allowing Rath to see the clean-shaven lower portion of his face.

Rath nodded. "Thanks for getting in touch."

The man crossed his arms. "I believe I told you that if our paths crossed again, it would go poorly for you."

"You did. I believed you. But I need help."

"Why do you think I would help you?"

He shrugged. "Okay if I sit?"

The man nodded, and Rath dropped to sit cross-legged on the floor. Amadeo crouched, which was nice because staring up at him was uncomfortable. Rath asked, "Seen the movie *Ronin?*"

"Of course."

Rath nodded. "Movie says, 'The warrior code. The delight in the battle. Also something more. You understand there is something outside yourself that you have to serve.' That's you. *You* understand."

Amadeo growled, "Movie quotes aren't reality."

He shrugged. "Nonetheless, accurate. You've proven that in the past."

The man released a soft sigh. "Believe what you want. It doesn't change the reality of the situation. So, what's so important you would court death to involve me in it?"

"Artifacts."

"You mean Rhazdon artifacts."

Rath nodded. "Yep. My team is collecting them. Trying to protect them from bad people. Need you to keep an eye out. Also, watch over Charlotte and Manny when possible."

Amadeo was quiet for a while, then he asked, "Let's say I do decide to get involved in your little project. What if I choose not to turn over the artifacts afterward?"

He shrugged. "Trust you to do the right thing."

A laugh escaped the man. "Kid, I'm a hired gun. I kill people for money."

Rath nodded. "Yes. But also, ronin."

Amadeo's lips twisted in a scowl. "You know what form my help would take."

Rath did. He was a killer, plain and simple. If he were to go after an artifact, no one involved other than him would be likely to come out alive. "I do understand. The artifacts are evil. They have to be collected, kept out of the hands of those who would use them to be horrible."

"What do I get in return?"

He shrugged and gave a small laugh. "What do you get the man who has everything? What do you want?"

Amadeo was quiet again for a time. "For each artifact I collect, or every time I have to intervene to protect your friends, you owe me a favor. I will name that favor at a later moment, and you will agree without argument."

"As long as it doesn't threaten my people or involve hurting innocents."

"I target enough criminals that we should be able to make it work. Since you're putting restrictions on me, you already owe me a favor for considering whether to be part of this and for not killing you. That favor also buys me checking in on your friends when I'm around. Including the blind man."

"You know about Chan?"

"Kid, I've been watching you all night. When I work out of a place, not much escapes my attention. Especially your launchpad on the cathedral, which I've known about since before we met."

Rath nodded. "Fair enough. Thank you for not killing me."

Amadeo rose. "No promises on that count. And troll, don't think you know me. The romantic image you have doesn't match reality. Thinking it does will get you killed."

"Maybe I know you better than you think I do. Maybe better than you do."

"Tell yourself whatever story you like, but do it on the

way out. Be real careful how you move with those weapons."

Rath did as instructed. As he walked out into the dugout and onto the playing field, he sighed, relief washing through him. *So, that's done. The cost isn't too high.* It had been a most excellent night, and if he could get to the top of the nearby parking garage, he'd be able to fly most of the way back to the cathedral before his portal home opened.

CHAPTER SIXTEEN

Kevin Serrano was in the locker room waiting when the portal opened and Tash stepped through. "About time."

She offered him an obscene gesture. "Calling me out of nowhere and expecting that I can simply disengage from the surveillance and investigation I'm doing is a little arrogant on your part."

"Not the first person to accuse me of that."

"What's the deal?" She pulled off her shirt as she opened her locker.

He was already in half of his gear, the basic uniform for the night's operation, but still had equipment to put on. He grabbed his belt and snapped the buckle. "We found a viable target. Doesn't look too hard, which makes it a good first run. A cult outpost in northern New Mexico. Makka is there at the moment to keep an eye on things. Once we join the rest of the team, we'll portal to his location."

Tash nodded, dressing at top speed. "Army folks coming along?"

Heaven forbid. Kevin shook his head. "Nope. The plan is to keep this op on the down-low. If it's possible to prevent them from knowing we're looking into the cults at all, that would be my strong preference. Only our people tonight, plus the mercenaries."

She finished buttoning her uniform top. "Seriously?"

He shrugged. "This is arguably tangential to our main operation. I want to keep it compartmentalized from the military and the oversight committee. Strictly need-to-know, and that means using hirelings is a benefit here."

He pulled on his vest, and she did the same, shaking her head. She complained, "I still think those guys are morons."

"They're the morons we have."

She pointed a long finger at him. "If you get me killed, I'm coming back to haunt you for your poor decision-making."

Kevin laughed. "Chances are if you get killed, I'm already dead so I won't care."

She closed her locker. "Fair point. Let's get a move on."

They strode together into the garage, where the rest of the team was waiting. He nodded, and the mercenary leader called his team's other magical. Shortly after that, they stood in a clearing in New Mexico with an expanse of stars overhead.

The non-magicals had night vision gear and suppressed weapons, along with abundant zip ties and injectors with knockout drugs inside. They planned to make as little noise as possible, get to whoever was leaving the cult, and take them prisoner or kill them.

The secondary objective was intelligence, either things

they might find during the op or taking people for questioning. He'd already arranged a place to transport them to, the basement of a building slated for demolition on the outskirts of D.C. The timetable for the building's demise would allow them to use it as an interrogation facility for a week or so, which was more time than they'd need. Its destruction would eliminate any evidence that could point to them, should that ever become a concern.

They all gathered in a circle, and Kevin said, "Lay it out for us."

Makka, dark-haired, dark-eyed, and dark uniformed, explained, "The techs did several drone overflights. What we're facing is basically a series of cottages that extend back into a ravine in a staggered arrangement. We anticipate the leader is probably in the rearmost cabin.

"Trees are all over the place, all the way in, and I've spotted sentries guarding the outside. They have a radio check-in every fifteen minutes or so. Not exactly punctual on that front, however."

The mercenary leader interrupted, "How much time until the next check?"

"Seven minutes, plus or minus how unprofessional they are." The man acknowledged the information with a nod, and Makka continued, "I think the only viable approach is to clear as we go. We don't want to leave people at our backs."

The merc agreed, "We definitely do not."

Kevin nodded. "So that's how it'll be, then." He turned to the mercenary leader. "I want you to detail one of your magicals back here, along with Makka and a team of non-magicals as rear guard. The rest of us will break into pairs, one magical and one not, and move forward. We'll coordinate attacks so the sentries can't support each other."

"Viable plan. Works for us."

Tash said, "Not like you have a choice, really."

The mercenary leader bristled at that, and Kevin interrupted, "Focus, people. Natasha and I will take the left. Your people will take the right."

Tash added, "Use magic to keep them quiet while you take them down. Prisoners are better than bodies."

The man snarled, "You don't need to tell us how to do our jobs."

She snarled back, "Based on prior experience, I do."

Kevin hissed, "Shut up, both of you, and move." He and Tash moved into position near the leftmost sentry, waiting for him to do his radio check. He whispered, "Why are you poking at them?"

"Because they're assholes led by a racist."

"Acknowledged. We need to work together right now. So put that in a box, shove it into the corner of your brain, and don't let it out until the op is over."

A small smile curved one side of her lips. "What if a few of them went down to friendly fire? Would that upset your friend Bradford?"

He slapped her lightly on the arm with the back of his hand. "Don't even think it. And he's not my friend. Only an evil that's unfortunately necessary at this particular moment."

The sentry spoke, his voice unintelligibly carrying as he reported in.

Tash said, "Move in three seconds." When they were in the field together, they worked as a team with no hierarchy, so he had no problem following her orders. He obeyed, and when their opponent spotted him, the man attempted to call a warning. However, the shimmering box that had appeared around his head stopped the sound from traveling through it.

Kevin dashed forward, kicked the man's legs out from under him, punched him a few times to give him something to think about, and pressed the injector against his leg and hit the trigger. The sentry's muscles softened as he dropped quickly into unconsciousness.

Tash crept up next to him and tied the sentry's hands and feet as Kevin pulled the radio from his belt and ear. He slipped the earpiece in to be aware of any unusual chatter that would suggest others had noticed them. A moment later, they received confirmation that the other side had taken down their sentry as well. He asked, "Any problems?"

"None. One person down, no injuries."

"Okay. Cabins are next. Makka, confirm rear guard is in place."

The magical's voice replied, "Confirmed. Way to leave me the boring job."

Kevin shook his head. "Somebody has to do it, and I trust you. Now, let's all cut the chatter and stay focused until we've finished. Just because they're likely amateurs doesn't mean they're not dangerous."

They continued moving as silently as the terrain allowed to the first cabin, which was about the size of a large shed, or maybe one of those tiny houses he'd seen on the Internet. Thermal imaging showed two bodies on different sides of the room, in horizontal positions. An additional figure was upright and appeared to be sitting next to the back wall. He asked Tash, "Ideas?"

She shrugged. "We break inside. I nail the one who's sitting with a solid blast of lightning. It should take him out immediately. You drug the one on the right before he can react, and we both deal with the third."

He nodded. "Will it be loud?"

"Only if we don't move fast enough."

"Can you do that trick with the magic box, only around the whole cabin?"

Tash shook her head. "Not while also using magic against the people inside. I think we'll need that, especially if he's sitting there with a gun or something."

Kevin frowned. "That seems like a rather unlikely scenario."

"But a possible one, you have to agree."

"Fair enough. Better safe than sorry. Let's do it."

They walked in a crouch first, then jogged in a crouch, and finally ran all-out toward the door. She turned the handle and shoved it open, and he thanked fate for doing him a solid in that they hadn't felt the need to lock it. The sitting man wasn't holding a gun but rather a deck of cards to play solitaire. Her lightning blast struck him full-on and dropped him to the floor in a clatter, his only reaction an expression of shock.

Kevin knelt and stabbed the injector into the chest of the sleeping figure on the right, who turned out to be a woman, and depressed the trigger. Another sizzle blew past him as Tash shocked the person in the other bed. They tied them up and waited for word from the other team. It came a moment later, a report of similar success. He glanced at his watch. "Ten minutes to the next check-in. Let's get a move on."

CHAPTER SEVENTEEN

Tash followed Kevin as he led the way to the next cabin. She was on edge, both because of the combat at hand and because of their alleged allies, the rental warriors he'd decided to include. She hadn't intended to get into a confrontation with them, but she couldn't get past their boss' attitude toward magicals.

The mercenaries' relative lack of effectiveness so far only increased her distaste for them. She was entirely glad that Kevin had separated the teams, so they were working on parallel tracks but not depending on one another.

Kevin raised a hand and froze, so she stopped at his side. "Two in the next cabin. Both look like they're sitting around a table. Probably the same layout as the other one."

"I should be able to blast them both without a problem."

He gestured ahead. "Have at it."

They repeated the process from the first cabin. She opened the door and launched a burst of lightning at the table's occupants. This time, it went wrong. Her electrical strike met a hastily raised shield, and the two figures rose from their chairs and rushed forward. Tash backpedaled and summoned her shield as one of the pair threw a fireball at them.

That apparently instinctive reaction by their enemy turned out to be a terrible idea. The flames exploded on her curved shadow barrier and lit the beds on both sides on fire. Kevin shouted, "I'm out," and she backed out the door, maintaining her shield. Right now, she had them trapped in the house, and her magical barrier would keep them from using the front door while the place burned. She extended her power and covered the two windows in the front as well. The glass in them shattered, but nothing came through. *If it was me, I'd be blasting through the walls with force magic to escape.*

She said as much to Kevin, and he nodded. "Guess our hope of going quiet is over now." He strode forward to the window, raised his rifle, and pulled the trigger twice, each depression sending three suppressed anti-magic rounds through her magical shield and whatever arcane protection the presumed cultists might have. She couldn't see what happened inside, but he lowered his weapon and turned away. "Let's get a move on."

She shook her head and followed, regretting that they'd had to kill them but still committed to their objective. Enemies rushed into view ahead from cabins on either side, and she blasted the nearest one with lightning. That figure was non-magical or at least failed to react in time because they fell to the ground, stunned.

Kevin shot one, smoothly shifted his barrel to the left, and dispatched another as more gunfire sounded from the right. She raced forward, grabbed her boss, and shouted, "Have the mercs handle the rest of the trash. We need to get to the big baddie before they run for it."

He fell into step beside her and gave the appropriate orders over the comm. "What do you think is waiting for us up there?"

"The heat signals the drones provided ahead of time had no relationship to what we found, so people moved around. Could be we'll find one person, could be we'll find ten. Probably somewhere in between." She skipped over a thick root, losing a half-step on her partner. "If we're lucky, maybe the leader is communing with a higher power and hasn't noticed what's going on."

Kevin snorted. "Yeah, I don't think our luck is quite that good."

She shrugged. "It's unlikely. About as likely as us finding Sheen or her team or anything about them here."

"Agreed."

As they neared the cabin, two heat signatures grew into solidity inside it. Both stood, one at the rear of the building and one near the door. Tash said, "Boss is probably in the back. I'll take care of him. "

"I'll help once I deal with the other one."

"Concentrate on not letting him kill you, please. If you die, I can't promise any of the mercenaries will survive to go home."

He laughed, but as they stopped running in favor of a more cautious approach, his amusement turned to concern. "You're not kidding, are you?"

She shook her head. "The more I ruminate on it, the

more they seem like cancer that needs to be eliminated if only because the temptation to use them is so great."

He nodded. "I understand your position. But don't. If you're that set on it, we'll find another way to bring them down. I need you too much for you to wind up in the crosshairs of someone bent on revenge."

"If you die, no promises. If I die, well then, sure, I agree."

Their discussion was interrupted by glass breaking as a fireball flew out of the cabin toward their position. She summoned a shield to protect them as a person bolted out the front door, headed at them in an all-out run. Kevin said, "Doesn't look crazy enough to be someone with an artifact."

Tash sent bolts of shadow at the figure, who called up a force shield in defense, but no tendrils emerged. "I agree. He's yours." She curved in an arc to avoid him as she dashed for the cabin door.

Kevin raised his rifle and squeezed off a three-round burst at the enemy rushing toward him. His foe jerked sideways suddenly—*as if by magic, the bastard*—and the rounds missed. Kevin tracked the weapon to the side, but before he could get the figure in his sights again, the man was too close. Kevin dove away, narrowly avoiding a cone of fire that would've burned him to a crisp.

He hit the ground, rolled on his shoulder, and came up at a run. As he angled for the cover of a nearby tree, he sensed the next attack coming and broke off that line, heading back toward the cottage. The tree burst into flames, limbs exploding from the concussive force of the fireball that had slammed into it. Heat washed over him, almost powerful enough to knock him over.

He turned and knelt, drawing the pistol from the holster on his thigh and steadying it across his opposite forearm. He pulled the trigger convulsively, shooting the weapon dry in only a few seconds. The first rounds struck true, but the remainder failed to penetrate the fallen tree limb the magical yanked up in front of him. Serrano ran to his right, hitting the button to release the magazine and ramming another in a moment later. He racked the slide, but his opponent forced him to dive again, this time to evade a cascade of lightning.

He didn't quite make it far enough away. Energy seared through his legs, sending his nerves and the muscles connected to them into agonizing convulsions. He brought the gun around and fired several more shots as he fell, but the magical interposed the tree limb again. Then he threw the heavy branch at Kevin and struck him in the legs, numbing them further and pinning him in place.

As the figure raised a hand to blast him into oblivion, shots came from Kevin's right as the mercenary leader stitched his attacker with bullets from knee to shoulder. The magical fell and Kevin dropped backward on the ground with a loud groan and waited for someone to give him a hand up.

Tash charged through the cabin door with a shield raised, and it caught the fire bolts thrown by the figure in the rear corner. He was tall and thin to the point of emaciation. Long hair fell around his face, and he looked for all the world like a skeletal Halloween decoration. However, the power that fueled his magic was nothing to joke about, and he continued throwing it at her, forcing her into a defensive posture as she put her energy into maintaining her shields against his assault.

That wouldn't have necessarily been a problem on its own since she could probably weather the attack until allies arrived. *Even if they are the damned mercenaries.* When the tentacles spiraled out of his chest and reached for her, the cumulative attack was too strong for her barriers to defend against. She allowed most of her shields to fall, focused mainly on keeping the tendrils at bay with a buckler on her arm, and used her other hand to hurl objects at him telekinetically.

The cabin held a bed, a chair, a table, and a small refrigerator. Each of those flew at him in turn, and he used his telekinesis to redirect or smash the incoming projectiles before they could reach him. The shadow tentacles from the artifact continued to harry her throughout the impromptu furniture hurling session.

When she had nothing left to throw, she blasted lightning at him. He extended a hand and somehow drew it into him, almost like he was using a spell that sucked away magical power. She felt the pull on her shield and wished for a moment that they could stop the battle so she could learn how to cast it.

He threw a force blast with his other hand, slamming

into her shins and knocking her legs out from under her. She careened to the floor, interposing an arm right before her face would've hit, and somehow managed to maintain her shield against the tendrils. Knowing an attack was imminent, she blasted force magic against the wall behind her, sending her skidding across the floor.

She pushed herself back to her feet, creating a full bubble around her again and reinforcing it with everything she had left. Then, knowing her plan to take the man prisoner had failed, she drew her pistol and pulled the trigger, sending three anti-magic rounds into his skull. He staggered for a moment, and she thought in horror that the artifact would somehow keep him animated to attack her. Additional rounds pierced his torso in response to that terrifying notion, but nothing so macabre happened.

He fell, and the artifact broke free and immediately rushed at her. She wrapped it in magic to stop it and used telekinesis to carry it outside with her. She ran to help Kevin up. "You okay?"

He grimaced. "Bumps and bruises. I'll get it checked out tomorrow." He looked behind her. "Had to kill him, then?"

"It was him or me." Her gaze flicked to the mercenary who stood nearby, and she continued, "It's never good for the other side when that happens."

Kevin shook his head. "Come with me. Let's get Makka to portal these prisoners away." He turned to the merc leader and ordered, "Your people sanitize the place. Burn it down. No evidence."

He nodded. "You got it."

When he was far enough away, Kevin asked, "You just can't help yourself, can you?"

Tash shook her head. "Apparently not. Might be better if you kept them on ops that don't include me from here on out."

He chuckled darkly. "I think for *their* safety, that's the best plan. Let's get our prisoners out of here and go home."

CHAPTER EIGHTEEN

Kevin closed the door to his office and let his shoulders slump. He'd been keeping up appearances in front of his people, but in truth, the battering his body had taken during the op was more painful than he admitted. He'd chosen to change in private rather than the locker room because he didn't want anyone to see the damage.

His bulletproof vest came off with no problem, so he moved on to the uniform shirt, then bent to undo the trousers. A bolt of pain shot through him and stole his breath away, and he decided he could keep wearing those and the boots until he got home. He shrugged into a clean t-shirt, left it untucked, and added a button-down casual top over it. He threw his gear into the corner, muttering, "I'll deal with it tomorrow."

He headed for the operations room, his final stop before heading home. Cassandra held down the fort, overseeing surveillance efforts on a different suspected cult site. He wasn't sure how often the woman slept or how much time she spent away from the office but imagined both numbers were probably low.

She said, "Nothing to worry about here, boss. Drones show a normal response to the fires in New Mexico, and there's no chatter mentioning us anywhere on social."

He nodded. "The artifact?"

"Locked in secure containment in the basement. Before you ask, the prisoners are under control as well. So you can go home and get some sleep. You look beat."

He chuckled. "I am, indeed. Good advice. Maybe *you* should take it yourself. Not that I would suggest you look any particular way."

She shrugged. "I love what I do."

He shook his head and waved as he exited. His car was warm and waiting to deliver him home, and he allowed the autonomous functionality to handle the piloting while he closed his eyes in the driver's seat. The car alerted him to their arrival with a series of chimes, waking him from a light doze, and he climbed out with a groan.

His house was entirely ordinary, a small single-family residence in the suburbs perfectly suited for his needs. He didn't know his neighbors, they didn't know him, and that seemed to suit everyone just fine. He walked up the small set of stairs to the front door, unlocked it with both key and thumbprint, and stepped across the threshold.

Three steps inside, his vision was cut off by a bag shoved over his head. Hands grabbed his arms from either side, and punches landed on his body, slamming into already bruised flesh. He was wrestled to the floor and heard the sound of the injector an instant before he felt the needle's pinch. A moment later, even the minimal light that made it through the weave of the blindfold went dark.

He came slowly awake, noting the sounds of people talking around him. A voice said, "He's up," and someone ripped the bag off his head. He blinked in the bright lights and saw a large, featureless room filled with stacked crates marked with military stencils. *It looks like a storage facility.*

His hands were bound behind him with a nylon tie through the openings of the metal chair he sat on, leaving him unable to shift more than an inch or two. His feet were similarly bound to the chair's legs, which, when he shifted his weight, didn't move a bit.

A figure stepped in front of him, one he recognized— Colonel Nance of the U.S. Army. The man offered a lazy, arrogant smile. "Mr. Serrano. How lovely to see you again." He gestured, and a woman in fatigues brought over a metal chair. The colonel accepted it, spun it, and sat backward, facing him with his arms resting on the back. "So, it's been quite an adventurous evening for you."

"I'm sure I don't know what you're talking about."

Nance nodded, and someone previously unseen behind him stepped forward and punched him in the leg. Kevin grunted in pain, unable to stifle a reaction due to the unexpected agony. The other man said, "Let's try again. Quite an adventure you've had this evening, isn't it?"

He managed a grim laugh. "Oh yeah, I remember now. Yes, quite."

Nance smiled genially. "Better. So, going after the cults, huh?"

Kevin gave as much of a shrug as his bound hands allowed. "If Sheen's after them, there must be a reason."

The Army officer stared into his eyes. "Power. Power is the reason. To that end, I'd like you to hand over the artifact you collected to us."

"Why would I do that?"

"Because we can use it, and you can't. Because we have the authority to use it, and you don't. Mostly, because I'm *telling* you to do it, and if you're under the mistaken impression I'm subordinate to you, it's time you understand that isn't the case."

"I thought of us more as peers," Kevin replied as a delaying tactic. *Although I don't know what the hell I'm delaying for. I'm sure they have a jammer going so no one can track my cell phone if I even still have it.*

Nance shook his head. "Nothing of the sort. You're a tool. I'm the craftsman. It's convenient for us to associate at this time, but I have a *lot* of tools. If one becomes problematic, I'll find another. So, please call your base and authorize them to release the artifact to my people."

"I'm not going to do that without the agreement of the oversight committee."

Nance snorted. "Oversight committee. Ha. They're more useless than you are and less valuable, which is saying something. I don't answer to them. As near as I can tell, you don't really either. So, call your people."

"I won't."

Nance raised a hand and pinched the bridge of his nose. "Listen. We're both professionals here. This nonsense doesn't suit us. If you don't call them in the next thirty seconds, I'll send my people in, kill everyone in the base, find the artifact, and burn the building down to hide the evidence. Your folks don't have a chance against our magical soldiers. You know it."

The officer lifted his head and stared into Kevin's eyes, and he saw the commitment there. "So, do you want the phone or not?"

Kevin scowled. "Give it to me."

Nance gestured, and someone brought his phone. As it came into his field of view, he discovered they'd managed to unlock it, which was concerning. The subordinate hit the button marked Cassandra, who was the person he would've called, and put it up to his ear. The colonel warned, "Any code, they all die and so do you."

He nodded. The woman's voice answered. "Hello?"

"Cass. It's Kevin. I was about to fall asleep, and I remembered something. I have an agreement with the Army to turn over the artifact to them. They'll be there shortly to pick it up."

"I thought you were keeping them out of it."

He suppressed a sigh at her insight. "Yeah, that was a cover story. Wheels within wheels, you know how it is. When they show up, let them have it."

"Okay. You got it, boss." The tone in her voice made him think she'd be investigating his whereabouts after the call.

When they'd hung up, the phone disappeared from view again. Nance asked, "So. Why the secrecy? I thought we were friends."

"You have secrets. I have secrets. That's how it goes."

"How did the mercenaries work out this time?"

Kevin tried to keep his face neutral, but he was sure he'd flinched, at least a little. *How the hell do they know about that? How the hell do they know about* any *of this? These bastards suck.* "It was a valuable test for them. They did better than on the first outing. Not as good as your folks, though."

Nance nodded. "That's because Bradford is an asshole and an idiot. You should remember that if this notion ever enters your brain again."

"Yeah. Will do," Serrano muttered.

"So, your objective was the artifact?"

Again, he tried to keep control, and again, he figured he might've failed. "Yeah, that's all."

Nance nodded, and another person from behind him on the other side stepped forward and punched him in that leg. He howled this time in a mix of pain and anger. *However impressive those bruises would have been, they'll be much more so now.* The officer asked, "So, you were only going for the artifact?"

He sighed. "And information. Still trying to figure out the cults to get us to Sheen."

"We'll want whatever you found."

"There was nothing at the scene."

Nance glared at him. "You surely took prisoners, right?"

Kevin let out a long sigh. "Yeah. We did." He provided the address and asked them if he could call and inform his people to release the captives rather than fight to keep them, too. They gave him that courtesy then dropped the bag back over his head.

Nance said, "It's been good working with you this evening, Mr. Serrano. If you try to cut us out of the loop again, there won't be a conversation. Only decisive action." He felt the expected prick of a needle, and blackness descended.

CHAPTER NINETEEN

Cara paused on the corner of Orleans and Dauphine in New Orleans' French Quarter and pretended to look at her phone for directions. She muttered, "They just turned down on St. Peter."

Anik replied, "I'll pick them up at the next intersection."

Cara crossed the street in a different direction than their quarry had. She and her partner had watched and waited, playing the role of tourists while carefully listening to conversations around them, frequenting the spots and events they thought might be most likely to draw a cult presence.

They'd finally gotten a break during a rally in Jackson Square, where a fringe group of magicals who'd been very loud on the national political scene about discrimination issues shared their views with a large crowd of magicals, non-magicals, and tourists of both kinds.

They'd noted one person in particular who gave off a condescending vibe toward the speakers and their message, and that had struck both of them individually as odd. Now, they followed to see if it was something or nothing.

Anik said, "Got her. Heading down Bourbon." Cara walked in the direction that would keep her parallel to their target's path. She and Anik were both dressed as tourists, in simple shorts, t-shirts, and tennis shoes. She wore a big floppy hat she could ditch at any moment, if necessary, and he had a ball cap in his pocket he could don if in need of a quick change.

Her chance of remaining undiscovered was high, thanks to her illusion necklace. If necessary, she could dash out of sight and alter her face in an instant. It wouldn't stand up to touch or magical inspection, but for this sort of surveillance, the magical item was perfect. If Anik felt threatened, he would simply fade, and she would follow as a different person.

Anik said, "Coming back toward you."

She replied, "Think she made us?"

"Doubtful. I can't see how."

"Okay, you follow. I'm going to walk past."

Cara made the turn to bring her face-to-face with their quarry. As they approached each other, she got her best look so far at the woman. She was of average height, wearing black shorts that were a little more revealing than Cara would've been comfortable in. A white tank with an artistically faded silkscreened image of Fidel Castro hung loosely on her thin frame, and a black bob finished it off.

The general look landed somewhere between PTA mom and rebellious punk, the latter reinforced by the tattoos that covered both of the woman's arms and the part of her chest that was visible between the straps of her shirt.

Cara shifted her gaze from the woman's face to the tattoos, which was likely a common occurrence. They were beautiful, one arm wrapped in depictions of marine life, the other painted with things that flew, birds, dragons, and the like. The tattoos that disappeared under her shirt seemed to be nature-themed as well. She smiled at their target in passing but received no reaction.

Anik asked, "Anything?"

She shook her head as she approached her partner, trailing the subject. He said, "She stopped. Now I'm going to walk by."

Cara didn't look back but waited until she reached the corner and crossed to the opposite side of the street she'd been walking along. In her peripheral vision, she saw Anik pass the woman, who was knocking on the entrance of a business. The façade above it proclaimed "Witches' Moon" and had a cartoonish logo of the moon, with the silhouette of a witch in a pointy hat flying on a broom covering half of it. The door opened, and their quarry went inside. She asked, "See anything with a vantage on it?"

He replied, "There's a frozen drink bar here with an open door, looking diagonally at it, more or less."

Cara sighed. Of all the alcoholic beverages she might want to enjoy in New Orleans, the generic frozen drinks that came out of the continuous mix cooling containers weren't high on her list. They enticed tourists who wanted to walk along Bourbon Street with giant drinks in their hands, competing for who could fall last. Still, she was willing to sacrifice for the job, and it would be refreshing, at least. "Meet you there in five."

They watched through the afternoon and into the evening, but the woman failed to resurface. As darkness began to drive away the last vestiges of the sun, more people passed through that small entrance. They had noted a much larger garage door set beside it that the owner could raise to allow entrance. It became clear they would have to go inside if they wanted to learn anything further that day, so they took it in shifts to head back to their hotel and change, then returned to watch.

By nine o'clock, music was blasting out onto the street through that larger opening, a live band playing hard rock with the occasional power ballad from the seventies mixed in. Cara had left her illusion necklace behind, fearing that the magical telltale would give them away. As they walked into the club, it became clear that they needn't have bothered. Magic was everywhere inside, making the air heavy with power.

Cara lacked the necessary level of sophistication to separate what spells might be at work. Still, it didn't take a genius to know that the pyrotechnics overhead were illusory or that some of the fabulously glowing costumes around were as well.

They pushed through the crowd toward the bar and grabbed a drink of the house special witches' brew, which appeared to be nine different types of alcohol mixed in random amounts with a sheen of cinnamon on top. She sipped, grimaced, and resolved not to do that again. Anik laughed at her expression. "It's not that bad."

She shook her head. "It is. It *really* is. It's like they

grabbed whatever they had left over from last night, dumped it indiscriminately into a cauldron, and called it a drink."

He grinned. "I've had worse at frat parties, for sure."

The band finished the song, and the crowd applauded enthusiastically. She asked, "Think our best plan might be to wander past the tables? See if we can pick anything up?" The place was loud, but their comms would help filter the noise if they trained their wrist microphones at their targets.

"I don't have a better idea."

They sauntered through the club, looking as if they had no particular destination. Tables they passed held obvious magicals, elves and dwarves, plus the occasional gnome. Several people gripped wands or had them conspicuously displayed as part of their outfits, but she had no way of knowing if they were functional or costume implements. The conversation at several was enlightening, although they only got snippets as they continued their journey.

One table spoke of a gathering of some kind. Another talked of the Mambo, which seemed like a definitive lead until Cara remembered that New Orleans was home for voodoo, and that title was present in their culture. After an hour of mingling, her head was pounding from the music, and she was about ready to call it a night. Then, Anik said, "Very slowly, look to your left."

She complied and saw only a press of people. A moment later, the crowd's motion gave her a line of sight to a person she recognized. A person she'd last seen at the side of Maîtresse Mambo Severine Eschete. The male member of a pair of different-gendered twins.

That sighting alone would've been a success, but it got even better. The man was working the crowd but also speaking with the workers, striding confidently behind the bar where no one moved to stop him. It was obvious he had a role in the place, either as a worker, owner, or something. It meant they'd finally found a real lead on the cult. She said, "We need to trail him."

"Could be difficult. He might use magic rather than walking."

She sighed. "Too true. Okay, we watch. I'll step outside and talk to Kayleigh, see if we can get some drones up to assist."

"Don't lie. You're going outside to sip more of that drink where I can't see you."

Cara laughed. "Oh yeah. That's definitely it. Moron." She headed for the exit with his laughter in her ear.

CHAPTER TWENTY

Deacon replied, "I don't think that's a good idea, Hank." He was seated at his computer in the Las Vegas condo he and Kayleigh had rented, a generic apartment in a tall tower near the center of the Strip. They'd chosen it for anonymity, easy access to food, and the high-powered fiber line that connected the expensive residences to the web.

Kayleigh walked into their shared office with a bag of Doritos in her hand and mumbled around a mouthful, "What's not a good idea?"

Hank's voice came out of Deacon's computer speakers, which was notable because it meant he wasn't using the team's comms for this discussion but had called on a phone. "The bus."

Kayleigh laughed, expelling part of a chip. "You know the boss *specifically* said no to that, right?"

"She said I couldn't go after it. She didn't say a thing about *Deacon* checking things out."

The infomancer replied, "Okay, that's technically accurate. Which, if I use it as an excuse with Diana, will *not* save me from getting my ass kicked. Tell you what. I'll take a look at the situation, see if I think I can get in and out without detection. If I have reasonably high confidence for success, I'll do it. If not, I'll inform you, and you'll agree to shut the hell up about it until the boss gives the go-ahead."

Hank's voice suggested he'd be as likely to give up the argument as he would be to give up breathing, but he agreed, "Okay. That sounds acceptable, for the moment at least."

Deacon shook his head in exasperation. "Okay. Stay out of trouble. Let us know what you need to secure the next location."

"Will do." Hank signed off. Kayleigh popped into her computer chair, which was diagonal to Deacon's right.

He swiveled to face her. "So, what do you think about it?"

"I think it's going to tick off the boss when she finds out."

"It might be worth it, though. Hank's not wrong that having our rolling armory among our assets would be a definite bonus."

Kayleigh shrugged. "That's very geographic thinking. We don't know where our next challenge will be. Could turn out that the bus is too far away to play a role. Not to mention the price of fuel these days."

He laughed. "Well, get in there and find me some more government accounts to hack."

She rolled her eyes. "As if they're infinite, or something."

"You're too good at your job. People expect you to work miracles. So, you know, go do that."

She frowned at him suspiciously. "You'd decided to do it before Hank hung up, hadn't you?"

"Like I said, you're good."

Going after information about the bus would be dangerous, no question about it. The team had very explicit ties to that asset, which meant Kevin Serrano would have to know about it. *That* meant Deacon's best way to find out about its current status was to go up against Serrano's team directly.

On the one hand, he relished the idea. The low-level back and forth over the worm he'd tried to implant had been amusing, but that game had run its course.

He knew Serrano's team included skilled infomancers. So, he'd have to be extra careful in all respects. He spent the day updating and refining his programs, ensuring they were as sharp as they could be on offense and as protective as they could be on defense.

He had a wide array of distraction and deception options queued up because the one thing he absolutely didn't want was the enemy tracing him back to the condo. *No way in hell I'm building yet another system in another place. I'd almost rather let them capture me.*

Deacon chuckled inwardly at his dramatic pettiness and focused on his demanding task. He pulled a six-pack of soda from the small refrigerator on the left-hand side of his computer desk and put it on the modest table next to it.

He popped the top on a can, drained it, and tossed the empty at the recycling bin across the room. It hit the wall above the toy basketball net Kayleigh had mounted there, then bounced off the rim and fell through to land in the bin. He enthused, "Score."

"Feel good about it while you can because that's the *only* way you're going to score."

He laughed. "Woo, harsh burn. You're just mad because you can't come along. Don't pretend to have some moral high ground. Because whatever moral ground you're on, it's probably subterranean."

She spun slowly in her chair to face him, stuck her tongue out, raised a middle finger, then rotated back. He laughed again, louder. "Classy, Kayleigh. Real classy."

She didn't reply, which was how their teasing sessions usually ended. He'd push forever, and she was too smart to let him.

He refocused on the task at hand and sent his magic into his rig. Speed would be of the essence once he made contact with the system, but for now he had time to move a little slower, to admire the computerized landscape with its vector lines and bright colors. He knew how to find Serrano's servers because the infomancers who used them hadn't been particularly concerned with protecting their virtual location by lack of knowledge.

No, they'll have really solid defenses up. Or maybe they're playing with me, and it's simply a way to entice me to attack some closed system that's a huge trap.

His firewalls were up, and nothing was going to compromise his system unless he gave it plenty of time to do it, which he definitely wouldn't do. If he couldn't get in and out in a few minutes in real-time, he'd abandon the effort. He was willing to face the boss's anger while delivering a successful report. He *didn't* want to have to tell her he'd broken security and allowed Serrano's people a line to their location. That wouldn't do it all.

"Okay, Deacon, quit dilly-dallying and get to work." He dove into the enemy's system and crashed through the first defenses without detection. The outermost layer was to keep basic viruses out. It could never stand up to an infomancer. Neither would the two underneath it, each addressing a more sophisticated form of conventional attack.

The first real resistance appeared five layers deep, and he paused momentarily to assess its strength. He concluded that he couldn't cut through it as he had the others but would have to engage it.

He gave the commands, and the virtual reality around him flickered and resolved into a video arcade. His avatar stood in front of the game *Spy Hunter*, which had always been one of his favorites. It had an airplane-style steering wheel, a foot pedal for the accelerator, a trigger under each index finger, and a button under each thumb.

His car was already in motion, and he steered it around obstacles. Slower and faster-moving vehicles appeared in his way or blasted up along the road he was on from the bottom of the screen. He avoided all of them, deploying smoke with the push of one button and a sheen of oil to make the car behind him crash with another. A rammer came at him from above, and he triggered a missile, which shot out and impacted the enemy.

He saw a lane leaving the main road to the left. It ended

in a familiar building, and as his car went through, it turned into a speedboat. He piloted it through the blue water that ran beside the road. When he hit the oil release button, it not only fell out of the rear of his boat but caught fire, immolating the nearest threat.

He fired another missile, this time at a helicopter, and steered out of the water and onto the road. He knew the game well, which meant two things. First, that he presumably wouldn't have too much trouble beating it, and second, that he was likely only facing artificial intelligences at the moment.

An enemy infomancer would either be more skilled or would've changed the scenario to deviate further from Deacon's preferences. As it was, when he thought that a speedboat would be a good idea, the opportunity to switch to one showed up. When he wanted to get back on land, that opportunity also appeared.

He ran out of missiles, and a supply truck showed up immediately. He drove his vehicle onto the lowered ramp and into the tractor-trailer, then back out a moment later, rearmed and refueled. After another minute of playing, he'd figured out what he had to do. When next he turned into a speedboat, he wrenched the wheel to the left, turning the boat in a direction it shouldn't have been able to go by the game's rules.

It traveled that way for a few moments. Then a helicopter arrived to herd him back into place. He destroyed it with a missile and did the same to the next one that came. Another wave appeared, and he slewed the boat, whipping it in a circle to deposit oil and setting it ablaze. When his screen was clear of enemies, the surroundings shattered, and he expected to see an interface that would let him access the data he wanted.

Instead, a different game solidified around him. He muttered, "Of course they'd have an infomancer watching over the place. All right, let's go."

CHAPTER TWENTY-ONE

The game wasn't one of Deacon's favorites. It was a two-dimensional platformer similar to *Donkey Kong*, which he was still annoyed about having had to play. This one involved riding an ostrich, or something that at least looked like one, and flying around on it trying to defeat other people atop bird creatures. Everyone was dressed in armor and wielded a lance, which was ironic because if you rammed someone head-on with it, you would almost certainly die.

The key to the game was dropping on opponents from above and collecting the eggs released by the defeated before they could hatch into more enemies. He wasn't sure what the success condition of this particular simulation would be. With some games, like *Donkey Kong*, the objective was fairly clear. If it followed the original in any way other than mechanics, it would probably be to survive sequential waves of bad guys until he reached and conquered an end boss.

The knowledge that another infomancer sat on the

other side of the figurative chessboard cast even that likelihood in doubt, however. Fighting AIs was predictable. Other infomancers, if they were any good at what they did, rarely were.

With a mental shrug, he willed his ostrich into the air. Normally, you had to repeatedly slap a button to flap the wings and gain altitude, but his magical computer interface was far more nuanced. He wanted it to happen, so it happened.

The simulation was real enough that he could smell the metal armor, and the lance in his hand was burdensomely heavy. He spotted an enemy, flapped over, and dropped on him. His mount knocked the figure from his bird, sending them out of the game.

Deacon swooped down and collected the egg immediately, before it could become a hazard, then flew evasively as two others tried to crush him from above. The simulation provided islands at various heights to give the players a place to land and rest from the constant button mashing. However, only one island was positioned on the lowest level, surrounded by molten lava. When he got near it trying to evade an attacker, the heat rising from it made him sweat.

Impressive simulation. He gave credit where credit was due.

His next attack run took him to the right-hand side of the playing field, where something unexpected happened. The normal game limited the players to one screen, and he'd prepared to turn and fly in the other direction. This one, however, scrolled. He flapped forward, dodging waves of enemies and navigating through a sky increasingly cluttered with islands. *So, it's part obstacle course, part combat. That's an interesting twist.* He filed that away to use in his future designs.

He defeated the wave, and text flashed, announcing another was inbound. A new screen loaded, and this one included explosives on the islands. It also revealed a more sophisticated enemy, bigger and visibly more threatening. He landed on one of them, which would've eliminated an adversary in the previous wave, and it didn't go away, which was alarming. That it vanished when he reflexively dropped onto it a second time was good, but the odds had now turned dramatically against him.

Deacon flapped wildly toward the right-hand side of the screen, trying to get more speed and stay in front of the ones pursuing him. He dipped to strike, then immediately fluttered up and dropped again to evade a counterattack. A hand of lava reached up to grab his bird, a feature he'd forgotten existed. He poured his will into flight, and they broke free, but now he was really in trouble. He dodged, dove, and evaded, but soon it was clear he only had a couple of moments left in the simulation.

Reluctantly, he triggered one of his failsafe programs. His character raised a hand and a round object that had never appeared in the original game materialized. He tossed in the air, and it detonated a second later, sending out a wave of power to knock all the enemy birds and their riders into oblivion.

It was, in fact, a simulated version of the Holy Hand Grenade from *Monty Python and the Holy Grail.* In reality, it was his system slamming a precise and damaging piece of code into the enemy server that caused it to perform a partial reset on the game. Such brute force attacks were never guaranteed to work, which was why he always tried to win within the scene rather than bashing it from outside.

Deacon got the sense that he now had the opposition infomancer's full attention when a huge knight appeared, levitating in midair and brandishing a pair of spiked flails that whipped in front of him in a blur of potential destruction. He readied his next best offensive attack to throw at the server, then discovered he didn't need it. The scenario shattered in a flare of brilliance, and when the light faded, he found himself in another.

He'd experienced this situation before. In the real world, his threat level had elevated to a point where a senior infomancer had taken over from the junior one he'd been facing. *And he was good, which isn't a positive sign for this fight.* Now he was in that defender's simulation.

A grin spread across his face as he realized it was one of his favorite games, *Mech Warrior*. He sat in the cockpit of a giant humanoid robot outfitted with assorted weapons and options for delivering mass destruction.

Other mechs fought all around him, but they were window dressing. This would ultimately be one-on-one against the enemy infomancer. His preferences had shaped the simulation, and he was in one of his favorite mechs. Missile launchers graced both shoulders, dual lasers ran along its left forearm, and a magnetic accelerator rifle replaced its right hand and arm.

He'd built his favored strategy around those specific weapons, and it had rarely failed him. As a bonus, the legs contained jump engines. A display caught his eye, and he saw that his mech was already damaged, its left chest plate at half armor. He muttered, "Well, that's just dirty pool. Scumbag."

The sensor suite was stock but still gave him a good picture of the surrounding mechs. They were universally smaller, except for one icon that ghosted in and out at the edge of his screen. *That'll be my target.*

A klaxon sounded, its tone indicating an inbound flight of enemy missiles. He ordered the mech to jump, and it crouched momentarily before soaring into the air on a burst of rocket fuel. Sparkling chaff ejected from the mech's shoulders, confusing several projectiles.

Others tried to turn to reacquire him but struck other mechs, or presumed allies intercepted them. One exploded near enough to send his mech off course. He quickly corrected the aerial stagger and guided the robot down to a thunderous landing. It squashed a treaded vehicle of an unknown kind, possibly a supply truck. He pounded forward, each step in the giant mech causing the ground around him to rumble and shake.

The enemy strode into view through the abundant smoke. It was one of the ones he disliked playing but also hated facing. Its primary weapon was a shoulder-mounted railgun that allowed the mech to deal devastating damage to its enemies at long range.

Since his opponent had mostly created the scenario, he had a distance to travel before he could bring his weapons into play. A metal bolt shot from the railgun, crossing the space between the enemy mech and his in a matter of seconds. He threw his robot to the side, overcompensating and falling to slide in the dirt. He forced himself up in time to move out of the way of the second projectile from the wicked weapon.

"Damn, that thing cycles fast." Most often, the railgun's weakness was its recharging period. The simulation didn't choose to respect that convention.

He ran in a serpentine to avoid more shots from the railgun. Another flight of missiles came in, and he reacted by launching himself into the air and deploying chaff again. He realized his mistake and cut the jump engines, but not in time. He'd sacrificed his maneuverability, and the railgun took advantage of it. The round smashed into the right side of his chest, fortunately. Had it hit the other, the metal rod would've passed through the compromised armor, pierced his engine, and exploded the mech.

As it was, it ruined his right chest armor and several of the servos underneath, making it impossible for him to rotate his mech's torso. He flicked switches to activate fire suppression and to eject the case of missile rounds on that side. A minor strike there could set them off, given the other damage. He wouldn't take that risk. Plus, the possibility that the strike had damaged the right shoulder launcher was high, and a misfire would similarly be quite bad for his mech's integrity.

He charged ahead, continuing the serpentine, and finally entered counterattack range. He launched the medium distance missiles from his left shoulder, and they spiraled in at the enemy. His opponent deployed chaff, distracting some of them. Several struck, though, hitting the mech in the legs as intended.

Deacon turned his robot, cursing at the lack of ability to swivel properly, and fired a ball of metal from the magnetic cannon that replaced his mech's right arm. It flew out at high speed and slammed into his enemy's thigh, blasting away more of the armor there. The third piece of his strategy, after the one-two punch of missile and magnetic, was the lasers. They carved into the already damaged spot, severing important connections and locking out the limb. The mech wobbled for a moment, but the operator showed his skill by keeping it upright.

Then his opponent demonstrated that mastery again by raising the railgun and firing it directly at the cockpit mounted in Deacon's mech's head.

His response was instantaneous, the only thing he could do. He slapped the self-destruct switch with one hand and the eject button with the other. The mech's skull shot off its body, which exploded a moment later.

The shockwave from the detonating mech sent him off course, and his skull-vehicle bashed into a hillside and rolled down, shaking Deacon hard enough to make his vision blurry within the simulation. He called up several programs, knowing his enemy would be moving in for the final kill. Then he popped the canopy and ran, activating his best defensive program.

The enemy infomancer hopefully wouldn't notice the slight wobble in Deacon's image as the program made the switch. A virtual version of his already virtual body continued its forward dash while his avatar became invisible and raced in a different direction.

He reached down for the packet on his virtual belt and started working its controls. In moments, he'd located a supply crate with a beacon, which in the simulation would represent the data he sought. He ran toward it, chuckling as the enemy infomancer stomped after the decoy.

Several minutes later in virtual time, which corresponded to seconds in the real world, Deacon logged out, the information he'd gone in to get safely downloaded. He activated his defensive AIs on the off chance the enemy had started a trace that might eventually lead them to him. Then he scrolled through the data and shook his head with a frown. "Well. Hank's not going to be happy."

CHAPTER TWENTY-TWO

Cara and Anik had trailed the twin that night and lucked out. The man had an apartment nearby, and they spent some time watching that, as well. It took a couple of days, but eventually, someone connected to the club and the twin's home visited the location that was their point of interest tonight. It was located far outside the French Quarter, in a block of condemned businesses Kayleigh's research revealed had been abandoned after flooding and never redeveloped.

Diana had decided the operation should be only magicals, so Cara was paired with Hank while the boss would work with Rath and Max. *So, mostly magical is more accurate, I guess.*

Cara guided them to the location and attached the network booster the others had brought with them to the outer wall. Over the comm, Deacon reported, "No computer system present, but there is a wireless signal. Ready to jam it on your order."

She looked at Diana, and the boss nodded. "Okay then, jam away."

Kayleigh softly sang, "We be jammin'. We be jammin'."

Cara sighed, wanting to laugh but knowing it wouldn't be the right response at the moment. Rath, however, had no such compunction and giggled. The troll had one hand wrapped in Max's fur and stood at Diana's side as if unwilling to let her get too far away from him.

Diana said, "Your show, Croft."

She gestured at the building. "Our target went through that door, so I guess we might as well do the same." She strode to it and turned the handle to find it locked. She pulled the electronic lock breaker from her belt, applied it, and moments later, it granted access. She led the way inside, the lowlight vision provided by her glasses rendering the space in artificial daylight. She wrinkled her nose. "Smells moldy."

Hank replied, "Yeah. Nasty. Looks like they broke out some walls in the back there to connect the structures."

She looked in the appropriate direction and had to agree. Someone had at least partially torn away each of the buildings' rear walls to create a sort of common courtyard in the center. Cracks showed in the roof above, and divots in the stone floor were obvious signs of where moisture had leaked through. The place looked old, smelled old, and the air tasted old.

Rath said, "Supplies."

She walked over to where he stood and confirmed he was correct. "Yeah. Food and water, all boxed up like it was shipped here in bulk. Not everything about this place is ancient."

The troll pointed up at a corner. "Camera."

"It's not wirelessly connected since I took that down. If you don't see a cable running out of it into the wall or something like that, it's nothing to worry about," Deacon advised.

The device looked more like a jerry-rigged baby monitor than a security device and had no cables attached. Cara muttered, "I don't think we're dealing with technological wizards here."

A scraping noise came from behind her, and she turned to see Hank pulling a large metal plate over the stone floor. The action revealed a ladder going down. She observed, "Seems as if using a heavy slab of metal to block off that access would make it hard to get back up once you were down there."

Diana nodded and met her gaze. "Kind of like putting locks on both sides of the doors in that other cult facility."

"I'm not sure I want to know what they're afraid of," Rath said.

Hank chuckled. "It's our job to find out. You and your dog aren't chicken, are you?"

"Good idea. Let's go get chicken nuggies. Triple order for Max and me. Forget about that ladder."

They all laughed, then Diana said, "Okay. I'm lead from here."

———

"Croft goes down first. Use the ladder, please." Her second-in-command rolled her eyes at the reminder of her poor decision on a past mission to jump down through a hole and trigger the magical trap at the bottom. "Next, Hercules. I'll lower Max halfway down, and Croft can take him the bottom half. Rath follows.

"Ironically, even though I said I was lead, I'll come down last and use telekinesis to move this plate most of the way back into place. I'll leave it far enough open that Rath can shrink and get through at need." The rest of them could portal, but neither of her partners could. She didn't have an easy backup plan for Max, unfortunately.

Rath nodded, then looked down at the Borzoi, perhaps regretting he'd argued Diana into letting the dog come along. How much risk to allow their canine companion to face was a fine line to walk.

They proceeded in order to the bottom, landing in a poorly hewn tunnel. Everything about the place was rough compared to the other cult locations they'd visited. *I wonder if that's because it was done recently, or in a hurry, or if they simply don't value this location the same way. Maybe it's not a worship spot for them?*

Cara remarked, "Now I have a bad feeling about this."

Diana replied, "Yeah, me too."

Hank said, "Seems like the kind of place you put something you want to forget."

Rath confirmed, "An oubliette. From *Labyrinth*."

Diana nodded. "Yeah, that's where my mind went as well. We need to be ready for anything."

They were all outfitted in their normal tactical gear, prepared to fight whatever they encountered. They still carried nonlethal grenades for the launchers and more at their belts if they came up against someone they needed to preserve. *Somehow, though, I don't think that's what we're likely to encounter down here.*

As they continued their advance, a door appeared, blocking their way. It fit imperfectly into the surrounding stonework. It also didn't offer enough room around the edges to get by, at least for anyone other than Rath at his smallest.

The bolt was on their side, as was the lock. They opened it and walked forward, arriving at a second door a short distance later. Cara observed, "Defensive positions."

"Yeah. Absolutely."

Rath said, "So, whoever created this place is as worried about what lies ahead as we are. That's good, right?"

Diana shook her head. "I'm not sure it is. Given how insane the cult members we've met so far have been, it's kind of alarming to think of what might frighten them enough to deploy this sort of defensive arrangement."

Cara ventured, "More skeletons, maybe?"

Hank replied, "Doubtful. Those weren't magical. They were technological. Whatever is going on in here, it's magic. You can feel it."

Diana paused and deliberately pushed her magic senses outward, an effort that took an unexpectedly large amount of power given her inexperience with it. Still, she noticed what the big man was talking about. A sense of malevolence came from farther ahead, and opening herself to its magic made her want to turn around, lock the doors behind her, and never come back. *Unfortunately, that's not the job I signed up to do.*

Her inner voice pointed out, "Technically, the government isn't paying you, so you're unemployed. And, for that matter, uninsured. You could totally walk away."

She considered the option again and discarded it. "Whatever lies ahead, it's better dealt with than not. Let's get a move on."

They arrived at another door, heavier than the first two, with multiple bolts securing it. Muffled sounds came through the barrier, moans, groans, and screeches, accompanied by occasional bursts of babble that made no sense.

Her glasses showed heat signatures on the opposite side, four of them, as near as she could make out. However, the way they clustered might conceal or suggest one that wasn't really there. "Ready?"

Each of her people replied in the affirmative, and Max gave a low chuff. "Okay then, let's do it." She pulled the bolts, threw open the door, and moved through it with her rifle raised to point at the beings inside.

Her glasses switched back to night vision mode, and she saw the targets for what they were—emaciated humanoid figures with shabby hair, long nails, and unwashed bodies. They were scabrous, disheveled, and in a word, disgusting. Their eyes glowed with madness, and an instant later, purple tendrils exploded from each of them, reaching for Diana and her allies.

CHAPTER TWENTY-THREE

Rath was in the rightmost position when the horrible creatures attacked, with Max by his side. He whipped up his batons and defended against the attacking tendrils, knowing that if one got through, the magic deflector in his vest would probably take care of it. The fact that his canine partner also wore one on his vest was both amusing and reassuring. The tentacles were fast, darting in from multiple angles and trying hard to break through his defenses.

Fortunately, Rath was faster. He whipped his batons in a defensive frenzy, occasionally striking one of the tendrils with the tip. When they connected, a spark snapped out, and that line of magical power withdrew from the battle, usually to be replaced a moment later by another.

He hissed, "Maxie, legs." Then he advanced on the creature, having to work even harder to keep the tentacles off him as he got closer. To his right, the dog took a curved path to sneak behind their foe. Rath grinned, knowing that they'd soon have the enemy under control.

Hank had been on the far left when their enemies moved to attack. He launched a stun grenade he'd already loaded in the under-barrel launcher. One of the tentacles slapped it out of the air, knocking it into a back corner, where it detonated harmlessly. He aimed at the thing's chest and pulled the trigger, and three rounds passed through the tendrils that tried to block them to bury themselves in his enemy's torso. The creature hissed, then screamed.

A corona of purple magic covered it, and when the power faded, the wounds were already healing. "What the hell," he growled and shot at it again. It appeared to have learned a lesson and grabbed fallen debris in the form of pieces of stone that had broken off from the wall, interposing them in the path of the bullets.

The improvised shields shattered on impact, but the tentacles simply gathered up more, creating a weaving defensive field. Hank continued to fire and warned, "Watch out. These things heal."

Cara had been next to Hank. She'd also tried a grenade with similar effect. Instead of trying to shoot her chosen monster, though, she'd drawn Angel and Demon and dashed at the enemy, hoping for a quick kill. It scuttled backward and away, forcing her to chase it.

The room was larger than she'd thought since the lowlight function of their glasses had a problem showing depth of field. The far wall was still too distant to see clearly, even with the improved light.

She chased, and tentacles snapped out at her. Her artifact weapons intercepted them, and the creature before her screeched in pain. Cara spun and ducked to evade a tendril that slashed over her head and popped back up to slice at it. She hastily changed tactics, calling up a shield from Demon as a sharp spear of stone flew at her eyes. She deflected it but then had to focus on continuing to avoid and block incoming projectiles.

When Hank announced his discovery, she groaned. *I can't even get close, and now it has to be a one-strike kill? Whoever is behind this needs to spend some quality time suffering.*

———

Diana had reflexively dropped her rifle and drawn Fury when the tentacles appeared. It was probably a testament to her overall mental state that at the moment of decision she selected the most comforting option. *So what? Sue me. I like the sword.* Fury's laughter tickled her mind. She swept the blade in short arcs to defend against the grasping tentacles, slashing them apart as she closed the distance to her foe.

The creature screeched and backpedaled, but she pressed, stepping into its path to angle it away from its allies. It suddenly rushed forward, trying to trap her in a bear hug so the tendrils could savage her back. She shifted Fury and forced her opponent to break off to avoid impaling itself. Her long sword gave her an advantage, at least against the creature's physical prowess. Its tentacles, though, came fast, furious, and seemingly unending.

The magic emanating from her foe was more powerful than she would've expected, having seen the state he was in. When Hank announced they had healing capability, she'd taken it in stride. When the thing started throwing stones at her, she adapted to that easily as well, shifting slightly to dodge or blasting them away with bursts of force where necessary. She grabbed one out of the air a moment after the tendrils threw it and hurled it back at her opponent's face.

Other tentacles reached up to intercept it, and she used the opportunity to send a wash of flame at the thing's feet with the tentacles occupied up above. It jumped aside, a tactical move to avoid the attack, showing no particular fear of the flames themselves. She said, "Burning doesn't scare them."

Cara snarled, "Neither does cold," having tried that attack. The bastard in front of her wouldn't allow her to close. Every time she got near, he flicked out tentacles like punches at her chest, and she had to retreat to avoid wasting the deflector in her vest.

If she'd been sure it would absorb the tendrils' full magic, allowing her to get close, she would've rushed the monster and ended things. *Hell, if I thought that I'd only get wounded, I'd still do it.* However, she couldn't be positive and couldn't indulge in heroics when the others might need her help.

It dispatched other tentacles to throw multiple projectiles at her, far too many to pick off individually, so she cocooned herself in a force shield. The creature responded by wrapping the shield in its tendrils, which appeared to be multiplying. Cara launched herself through the protective shell's top and into the air with a force blast against the floor, flew haphazardly into an empty area, and landed in a skid. She growled, "Okay, scumbag. Enough."

She thrust Angel into its scabbard, summoned a buckler with Demon, and lifted her rifle one-handed, holding down the trigger to send rounds at her foe. The tentacles focused on pulling up objects to block with, and she closed while it was so occupied. When the rifle ran dry, she let it drop and pulled out her pistol, continuing her forward march as bullets flew from it. Tendrils reached out to punch her and shattered her magic deflector, which cracked and fell away.

Finally, she was close enough. As the tendrils wrapped around her neck, she stabbed Demon into the thing's temple, then yanked the blade sideways and shoved it in as deep as it would go. The creature fell, and an artifact wriggled out of its chest. She locked the evil object down with magic and reloaded her weapons. "One down."

Hank replied, "Number two, about to be down."

He thought he saw a weakness in his opponent's strategy. It was attempting to hit him with its tentacles, an effort Hank frustrated with quick shields that intercepted them hard. The defense seemed to be working, and he'd concluded that however strong the thing might be magically it was physically weak.

If it attempted to hold its tendrils stiffly to stop him from rushing in, it got knocked off balance. If it let them go limp, he would get close enough to do damage. The only challenge was how to damage it so it couldn't heal before he could finish it off.

Fortunately, Hank had been in a lot of fights—*a lot,* a lot —and knew a dozen ways to pull that off with his bare hands. He set himself, summoned up the small amount of magic he'd managed to build from punching the tentacles with his shields, and rushed forward with a yell.

At first, the creature tried to resist, but as he knocked it off balance, the tendrils fell away. He charged in, and they snapped at him from the sides and the back, attacking his head, arms, and spine. The magic deflector took care of the first few, and the ones that got through weren't sufficient to stop his headlong rush.

He leapt into the air and brought his elbow around in a strike at the thing's throat. It lowered its chin, taking the blow there instead. Its jaw shattered, and it was momentarily stunned by the damage.

Hank skipped behind it, grabbed it by the neck, and yanked forward and down, snapping the monster's spine over his shoulder. He spun and twisted the neck for good measure, ensuring everything inside it would no longer function. The creature fell, and an artifact burst out of it. He captured it in a cocoon of force magic and checked to see if his allies needed assistance.

Max reached their foe's leg unnoticed while Rath kept the monster busy. The dog moved behind it and snapped his teeth down on the enemy's Achilles tendon, grabbing and tearing it. With a surprised screech, the enemy listed to the side and stumbled toward the floor. Hank had warned that it would heal quickly, so Rath had only two priorities: protecting Max and killing the thing.

He let his right-hand baton fall and dashed forward, using his left weapon to intercept the tentacles headed for Max. He shouted for the dog to run, and Max complied. The tendrils stretched after him, presenting Rath with a moment of decision where he had to choose between protecting his partner or ending the fight. He judged that Max had accepted the risk, just like he had, and hoped the deflector in his vest would be enough.

Instead of blocking the tentacles seeking the dog, Rath slapped down the ones defending against him and leapt into the air. As he flew, he drew the knife with the fire etchings from its sheath. Diana had charged them all up, but they hadn't found a good opportunity to test their power in any useful way yet. *This will be an excellent test.* He threw the blade true, and it stabbed deeply into the thing's throat.

The monster gasped at the impact, then fire burst from the weapon, covering the creature. Its gasp turned into a wail of agony or anger as the flames consumed it. The artifact emerged from the conflagration and headed for Max. Rath hurled blades at it to force it off course and shouted, "Help Max. Artifact."

Diana continued battling her foe, trying out lightning, but it dodged again. The creature used its tentacles well, shifting them between shield and offense, interposing them to stop her attacks and keep her at bay. When Rath shouted, she jerked her head to the side and saw the situation, then used a force blast to redirect the artifact toward her second-in-command. She hollered, "Croft, incoming," and dove away from the tendrils that sought her.

Cara replied, "On it," and Diana realized hers was the only enemy still standing. With a curse, she said, "All right, you jerk. It's you and me." Then, contradicting herself after a moment's consideration, she added, "Hercules, Rambo, little help." Gunfire came from her left, and a dagger flew in from her right.

The thing lifted blocks of stone in each direction to defend against it, and she charged forward, holding Fury at her side almost like a retracted lance. It stuck out more tendrils to stop her, but they crashed against her deflector and dissipated. She stabbed with all her power and momentum and ran it through the heart, burying the sword to the hilt. Then she twisted the weapon and ripped it out the thing's side. The artifact emerged, and she locked it down with a force cube.

Panting, she checked to be sure her allies were safe. Hank said, "Well. *That* was awful."

Cara replied, "I can't believe it went for Max. What would an animal with an artifact be like?"

Diana shook her head. "I don't think we want to find

out. Rambo, buddy, maybe we need to leave Max at home sometimes."

The troll nodded. "Yeah. Good call." He looked down at the dog. "Sorry, buddy. Artifacts too dangerous. You'll have to be home guard for these things." Max barked, seemingly unconcerned, and Rath laughed. "Best dog ever."

CHAPTER TWENTY-FOUR

The setup in the warehouse was nothing short of bleak, but at the very least they weren't risking Ruby's involvement any longer. Hank and Tony had set up a portable generator, which purred quietly in the corner. Electrical lines snaked from it to some work lights on stands around the circle of chairs and the space heater in the center. There were a few other scattered lights, but overall, it wasn't a place they would want to hang out in for very long.

After their adventure in New Orleans, Diana had decided it was time everyone got together in person for a chat. She'd even called in Sloan and Bryant, choosing not to closely examine her motivations for bringing her boyfriend back to safety.

She took one last look around at her people and smiled at them. "Okay. So, long story short on New Orleans, we found the monsters in the basement. They were pretty much *literal* monsters—people driven insane by artifacts, living like animals. More to the point, they were being *kept* like animals, fed and watered, not simply abandoned. It must be a failed experiment by the cult or something."

Cara nodded. "You all should've seen them. They were just wrong." She gave a dramatic shudder.

Rath was sitting cross-legged on the floor next to the Borzoi. He added, "Max says they taste bad, too." Everyone laughed at that.

Diana summed up that adventure by saying, "The good news is they're gone, and we have some artifacts to keep track of. Our imminent decision is where to keep these artifacts and store any others we come across. But first, Bryant, want to give us an update on your stupidity?"

Her boyfriend was seated opposite her and offered a playful scowl in response. "Well, my stupidity, as you call it, has not yet come to fruition with any actual information."

Diana interrupted, "So you're admitting it was stupid."

"I'm doing no such thing. In the spy business, you have to sow seeds and let them grow. We can't all be all 'Kick in the door, smash everything inside' all the time like you."

Hank countered, "Direct action is where it's at."

Sloan interjected, "I disagree. I'm in much the same situation as Bryant. I've worked my way into the group, nominally speaking, but haven't yet seen its real face. Hopefully, I'll know more soon.

"I have to say, though, the guy in charge in Pittsburgh seems completely normal, for lack of a better word. Like someone who could eventually become a televangelist, run a megachurch, or something. Forceful personality, great oratory style, but no particular sense of magic about him. I presume he has Oriceran blood, but he hasn't yet made it evident one way or the other."

Diana nodded. "Keep us informed. That seems much less stupid than Bryant's efforts." She smiled at her boyfriend. "Good deal. Okay, back to the artifacts. My first thought was the Paranormal Defense Agency."

Kayleigh replied, "Seriously?"

Diana gave a short laugh. "I know, right? Ironically, they're the only government group that doesn't seem to have an agenda regarding the artifacts. Like us, they only want to collect them and get them out of circulation. As near as I can tell, anyway."

Deacon asked, "Would the artifacts be better off on Oriceran? I mean, not to shove our problems literally off the planet, but it seems less likely Serrano and his people could get to them there."

Diana shook her head. "Nylotte is working an artifact angle there, so she's bringing some together as well. Better that they stay split up. Sure, we could store them in all sorts of other places on Oriceran, but leaving them unguarded isn't a great option either."

Cara suggested, "One of the kemanas?"

Bryant replied, "Security concern. We'd be counting on our enemies not figuring out where to look since we don't have an existing trusted hiding spot there. Probably not viable."

"I have an idea." Rath sang a few bars of the song from *The Little Mermaid,* "Under the Sea."

Diana laughed and grinned down at him. "Yeah, Cali is an option too, in New Atlantis. But one I'd prefer not to invoke right now. She says the cult is present down there, too, and it's a rather smaller haystack to hide the needle in than the entire country we have access to up here. Still, that's a good fallback, and we should probably visit to set that place up as a refuge, too."

Hank shrugged and leaned back in his chair, extending his long legs in front of him. "Seems like you have your mind made up on this one."

"You're not wrong. I wanted to see if a better idea might bubble up. For now, I think Ruby's bunker is the only place that offers both security and support to guard them. Does anyone disagree?"

Hank ventured, "If we had the bus—

Diana raised a hand as everyone burst into laughter. "Hold that thought, Hank. We aren't there yet. I know about the little adventure you sent Deacon on." He didn't look chagrined. No other voices chimed in. "Okay, Ruby's bunker it is. Assignments will stay the same, more or less, for now." She twisted to face the infomancer. "Deacon, want to share what you discovered?"

"Not surprisingly, our long-missed mobile armory is still in the same place where we left it. I found some data about how they've been trying to break into it, and it seems unlikely they'll succeed anytime soon. I'll admit I was surprised by how little effort they're putting into it, to be honest. I'd thought breaking in and taking it over would've been a major part of Serrano's plan. Only a few techs are assigned to the project, along with a couple of fairly unimpressive infomancers, according to their personnel records."

Hank grumbled, "So we know where it is, and we know it's still fully functional, or they'd be inside it already."

"Accurate. We also know it has sizable security

protecting it, although my data didn't give me any other details on that. Only a big-budget number for it."

"So, we're going to have to check it out."

Deacon nodded. "Yeah."

Cara asked, "Drones?"

Kayleigh shook her head. "We pulled some satellite imagery of the place. There's a drone screen operating around it."

Diana replied, "Meaning?"

"Meaning we won't get one of our drones anywhere close. It looked like the screen was several blocks out from the facility."

She frowned. "Did they add any external security other than the drones?"

Kayleigh replied, "Funny you should ask that. We can't tell. The satellite images we have access to have been electronically redacted to conceal the area. Anything within a block and a half range of the building is under a black box. We were lucky the screen was so far out, or we wouldn't have known about that, either."

Bryant frowned. "I've only ever heard of that happening for military bases."

Cara offered, "Same here."

Kayleigh shrugged. "I'm only delivering the news. I don't create it."

Hank said, "When we finish with the next warehouse, Tony and I can pop over and check it out."

Diana countered, "After you finish with the next warehouse, you'll move on to the one after that. You will most certainly *not* go anywhere near the bus."

He frowned and sat up. "It would be a serious asset to what we're doing."

"Would it? What if what we're doing is in Magic City? Are we supposed to wait three days for you to drive the bus over there? It's not like we have airlift capability anymore."

His frown deepened, and he drew in a breath to reply, but Diana raised a hand. "I'm screwing with you, Hank. We'll check it out, but you're not the one to do it. I need a more dispassionate view of the situation. Cara will go."

Her second-in-command sighed. "And here I thought that I would bask in the sun and have a day or two of R&R in New Orleans. You're a damn taskmaster, boss, is what you are."

Everyone laughed. Rath offered, "Could provide aerial support."

Diana shook her head. "Not with the drone screen. For all we know, those things carry arms. No, Cara has experience with being sneaky. We'll let her handle this since it plays to her strengths.

"Meanwhile, the rest of us will keep doing what we've been doing and resting up when we can. If going after the bus turns out to be a thing, we'll need to be at our best. Even if we decide not to pursue that angle, we certainly have to keep putting pressure on the cult, which means we'll all be headed back into action soon enough."

The group broke up, and she wound up in a small circle with Rath, Max, Kayleigh, and Deacon. Her blonde nemesis said, "Keeping the artifacts in Ruby's bunker is less than optimal."

She nodded. "I know. I'm not thrilled with it. Aside

from Rath's suggestion of New Atlantis, I don't see another viable option."

"They could stay with Deacon and me."

The infomancer signaled agreement, but Diana shook her head. "No. You might bring heat on yourselves with your actions. As much as I don't want to lose you, which I don't—I'm speaking specifically of Deacon here—I also don't want to lose the artifacts if I can avoid it."

Kayleigh stuck out her tongue at the insult. "You could draw Serrano to Ruby."

"He won't know."

The tech shook her head. "Dangerous. I hope you're right."

Diana grinned, feeling for the first time in a while like her team was back in control of the various situations they were running. "I'm always right."

CHAPTER TWENTY-FIVE

Cara hadn't set foot in Hampton Roads, Virginia, since they'd delivered the bus there before moving their operation to the vimana. Memory washed over her as she walked the streets several blocks away from her destination, meandering in the sunlight without any obvious purpose.

She'd dressed in clothes she wouldn't normally wear, leggings, sneakers, a ski jacket, and a sweater underneath. A bright red knit cap with a tassel on top hid her hair. So garbed, she was fairly certain no one would look at her and think, "Oh, that's a military person turned federal agent turned fugitive doing reconnaissance." At least, she hoped not.

The techs had done additional research and discovered a coffee shop with a sightline to the facility. She found the entrance where they'd promised it would be and headed inside, ordering a drink that suited her persona and involved pumps of things into coffee and foam with a sprinkle of grated chocolate on the top. *Okay, there might be some parts of this personality I can relate to.* While she usually drank her coffee black, she certainly wasn't averse to a little treat now and again.

The operation had more than one purpose. The primary goal was to figure out what to do about the bus. She was on Hank's side, but as Diana had said, she could approach it relatively dispassionately. Ideally, it would all work out, but if it couldn't, at least knowing that would allow them to check a box and move past it.

The second purpose was to test their comms' operation in magical mode. She sat at one of the stools in front of the bar that ran across the window and looked out. She muttered, "Okay, I have a visual." Her phone acted as the replacement interface for the belt pack she'd normally wear to relay signals to the tiny earpiece.

Kayleigh replied, "I have it, too."

So that's working, at least. She pulled a tablet from her large purse that now hung from a hook under the bar and opened it, casually tapping a few buttons. While it would look to any observer like an ordinary off-the-shelf device, it was an enhanced sensing package in disguise. She plugged in an external battery, which held more sensor components and provided power.

The screen flicked through various useless charts and graphs as she tapped it absently. Her attention was all for the display in her glasses, which gave her the sensor feed. She only had a cone view cross-section of the facility but could still make out a few important things. The magnified normal vision showed her cameras all around the building's perimeter, drones flying overhead, and that someone had added a chain-link fence topped with barbed wire as an outer defensive element.

The sensor switched to heat, and she got images from the drones nearby, but nothing from within the building. *Hmm. Interesting.* A figure walked slowly along a straight line on the nearer side of the structure, presumably a patrol. The next mode was electrical, and it showed spots that probably indicated sensor devices around the grounds. The building emanated an extremely faint signal of electrics but far less than one would expect. "They have some jamming going on here."

Kayleigh replied, "Our conclusion as well."

Cara's glasses switched back to magnified mode in time for her to see the patrol as it came into view. It was a single guard, walking casually, his head swiveling regularly from side to side, looking for trouble.

His black uniform lacked insignia, and he wore a bullet-proof vest and protective armor plates in other locations. A rifle was held across his chest, ready to be deployed at an instant's notice. She muttered, "That's not a casual rent-a-cop sentry."

"No, it isn't." After a moment, the tech continued, "Switch to signal detection again."

Cara complied and frowned once more at the nothing-ness in the center of the screen. "Equipment malfunction?"

Deacon joined the conversation. "Doubtful. Jamming. I'm sure they put it in place so we can't try to hack the bus from outside."

"Did you get anything else from your foray into the enemy servers that might prove useful?"

Deacon's frown was present in his tone. "No. I got the

data back, and it was full of holes. My run wasn't as successful as I'd hoped. That happens sometimes, but I have to admit, those folks didn't seem like they were skilled enough to pull that off."

"He's a little sore about it. Lots of stomping, occasionally throwing things," Kayleigh remarked.

Cara snorted but disguised it as a sneeze, trying not to laugh. "I totally understand. Did you get a sense of who the opposition is here?"

"Definitely Serrano's people. Some telltales signal the Army as well. I think the technicians are from NSA or Homeland. If I had to guess, the infomancers are from one of the academies. They're not going to succeed at their task."

Cara laughed again since Deacon's tone suggested the chance of them hacking the bus was about as likely as her walking on the moon in the next few days. "So, you're saying a breach is imminent?"

He snorted. "Maybe this century."

She grinned. "Hank's right to be proud of what he accomplished with this thing. You all were smart to reprogram it when the feds turned it over."

"The back doors they left in weren't all that well-hidden in the first place. Government contractors, probably a low bidder. They should've used the military for that part. At least they're committed."

Cara checked her watch. "We have about fifteen minutes before my test comes online. Do you want to do yours now?"

Kayleigh replied, "You don't think it will cause a problem with yours?"

"Nope. If it does kick them into a slightly higher level of alert, seeing how they react to mine in that situation will be useful. Go for it."

"All right. Stand by." A new window opened in her glasses, showing the feed from a drone hovering a couple of miles away from her position. It slid into motion on a heading that would bring it into contact with the drone screen.

She'd brought the commercial model with her and launched it earlier, and it had been in Kayleigh's hands since then. They were all curious to see what kind of drones were over the base and how they might react to the idea of an incursion. When it closed to within about eighty feet of the screen, it started to jerk and shudder.

Kayleigh reported, "Either jamming or maybe hack attempts, or both. I can't tell."

Deacon replied, "Me neither. If it *is* a hack, that's impressive work. I'm guessing jamming."

Kayleigh managed to keep it on target, but when the drone got too near what would be firing range for an armed version, three drones detached from the screen and surrounded theirs. The other craft made contact, which resulted in a lot of shaking and jarring of the image. Kayleigh reported, "I think they're stuck on it now. I can't break free."

The drone trio took theirs to the ground, and they saw a closed-top black, unmarked Jeep pull up a couple of moments later. "Disconnecting." The feed went dark.

Cara observed, "Aggressive response, but a safe one. They didn't simply blow it up or kill the electronics and let it fall on a passerby's skull below. That speaks to a certain level of restraint."

Kayleigh chuckled. "Hooray for minimum effort."

"Oops. Looks like my guy's early. Let's see how this one goes." Cara switched back to magnification to watch as a young man in jeans and layers of sweatshirts, one of them a hoodie that covered his hair, boldly walked up to the fence.

He called to one of the men inside, and the sentry walked over to him, the gun still in rest position across his chest. Her microphone wasn't good enough to pick up the words, even with the enhanced sensors, but she knew he'd be taunting the guard, asking if he could come in and use the restroom and generally making a nuisance of himself.

Kayleigh asked, "Is this a good idea for him?"

Cara snickered. "He'll say it's a fraternity stunt, and the best part is that it truly is. You have to go several levels deep, all the way to the national chapter, before you find our connection to it. Even then, it's only an old Army friend of mine. By the time they're able to trace that, he'll be in the clear if they don't tell him to go away in the first place."

The response was rather more serious than that. Another black Jeep pulled up, its occupants bundled him into it, and the gate opened to take him into the base. Cara sighed. "Well, this place looks about as impossible to get into as anything we've faced before. Not to mention the difficulty in driving the bus out of there if we happen to break through the defenses. It's a seriously bad idea."

"So you're guessing it'll be a no-go, then," Deacon replied.

Cara chuckled ruefully but quickly stifled it. "No. It means the boss is going to love the idea."

CHAPTER TWENTY-SIX

Bryant had returned to D.C. after the meeting and taken another nap since his healing body seemed to require more sleep than usual. Then he'd gotten up, slipped on his illusion necklace and some innocuous clothing, and headed out to make the rounds of his information drops. He did this every day he was in town, varying the order and sometimes skipping a few not to be overly predictable. Today, though, he had an even more specific reason to be out and about.

A post on the same cigar aficionados board as before had informed him a signal had been left but not provided a location. His contact was aware of a few of the information drops, although that probably wouldn't be how she passed this message. He and the representative had their system, different from his standard methods, and he'd verify those possibilities as a matter of course, as well.

He walked into the park, looking for a particular piece of trash stuck in a specific bush that would alert him to check one of the physical drops. Beyond that location, over a waist-high brick wall that enclosed the green space, he noticed a black van. It was taller than the most common versions, which had caught his eye.

More comfortable for people to sit inside if that's what's going on. He turned away from it, keeping his face neutral, and pulled his phone up to his ear as if he was speaking into it. "Hey, G."

A few moments later, Kayleigh's voice came through. "Yeah?"

"There's a black van parked near me. I'm pretty sure I saw it nearby a couple of days ago. Do you think you could bring in a drone to take a look?"

"Probably not a good idea. A commercial drone would attract attention, and if I used one of the new advanced military ones, that would draw a different kind of attention. They have two-stage transponders, one that classifies it as military and another that sends out a particular ID number.

"We've rigged each to turn off on command, but one without the other will be suspicious, and if it's not flagged as military in the first place, you can count on an aggressive response. People don't like it when you fly uncrewed vehicles near important buildings."

That makes sense. Damn it. "How about the traffic cameras?"

"Another no. Deke still has a hook into them, but their infomancers have been pushing hard to locate him and kick him out since we used them to track the vans and rescue you. They haven't found him yet, but the search continues. Boss told us not to access them unless it's critical. You don't sound like it's critical."

"It's not. Okay, thanks. For nothing." He laughed.

Kayleigh replied with sarcastic humor, "Don't mention it. Literally anytime. That's how much I care for you. Might not want to tell the boss. She's the jealous type."

He slipped the phone back into his pocket and moved the location into the "burn" column of his mental list of viable drop points. He wouldn't revisit it. *Who knows, the van could be nothing. Probably is nothing. Assuming that would be stupid, though.* He spent the next hour in unproductive wandering, employing subtle countersurveillance tricks to see if he'd acquired a tail.

When he was positive that he hadn't, he finally turned to pass a small restaurant that was one of the unique signals he shared with the representative. A sign in the window read, "Great job. Apply now. Hiring dishwasher. Start immediately." He didn't pause and spent another fifteen minutes on foot before stopping to buy a coffee to go from a café and summoning a car to take him back to his hotel.

The existence of the help wanted advertisement wasn't an indication that the restaurant had an opening to fill. It was a message from his contact that told him two things. The mention of a dishwasher gave him the meeting location. Hiring immediately meant she wanted to meet that night. If that hadn't been in there, it would've been the next day.

He slid open the closet and pulled the dry-cleaning wrap off his nicest suit. He donned the blue pinstripe with a white shirt and a stylish bowtie and slipped on a pair of newly shined shoes. The illusion necklace he would've liked to take wasn't appropriate to the venue, nor to the person they knew him as. He headed into the bathroom and changed his hairstyle, slicking it back severely and putting enough product in to ensure it would stay that way.

The meeting spot was exclusive, one of the many clubs in D.C. that catered to a very narrow clientele, all moneyed. He'd faked the credentials to get in long ago when he started working in town and had done the same with several other similar venues. Those connections existed specifically to meet with or recruit high-level contacts.

He'd used a couple of the businesses failing to secure recruits. Once that had happened, both contact and location landed in the "burn" column as well.

He ensured he had the proper identification loaded in his wallet, then nodded at the man in the mirror and headed for the lobby. The concierge summoned a car for him, and he instructed it to go to the Cosmos Club. The vehicle got him there in a little over a half-hour, thanks to annoying traffic snarls, which meant he had about twenty-five minutes before his guest would arrive. He would've preferred more to assess the other people inside for threats.

The building's exterior was unchanged. Wide slabs of off-white stone, each a couple of feet high, made up its first-level façade. The areas above held windows with fancy curtains, and behind those fabric panels lay private salons on the second floor and rooms for rent on the higher levels.

He'd never stayed there overnight, the cost being far too rich for the expense account he was on at the time.

Now, I could steal some more. Maybe I should consider that. Take a short, high-class vacation.

He climbed the small flight of steps to the front doors, which opened at his approach. He nodded at the uniformed bellhops on either side, whose costumes hearkened back to movies from the early nineteen hundreds. A man in a tuxedo presided behind a standing desk positioned near the entrance. He intoned with gravitas, "Welcome to the Cosmos Club."

"Thank you." Bryant handed over a thin metal rectangle, about the size of a standard credit card, that served as his identification. The man checked the engraved numbers against a leather-bound book, another historical affectation of the place. "It's been some time since we've seen you. Good to have you back."

The comment didn't sound suspicious, or at least not entirely so, but Bryant sensed the question in it and smiled. "I've been out of the country. Working on a project involving extending the longevity of satellites. Very hush-hush."

Something softened in the man's expression, and he nodded. "Of course."

"A guest will be joining me. Please escort her in when she arrives."

"Certainly, sir. Yvette will take your jacket, and Selena shall accompany you to the dining room." Two women in gowns that would've been appropriate at a presidential inaugural ball did so.

A tuxedoed server appeared at his table the moment he sat down. "Is some wine to your taste tonight, sir?"

He nodded. "Have the sommelier pick out a red. Something chewy, but not too heavy."

"Very good. Would you prefer to wait until your guest arrives before ordering?"

"Yes, thank you."

The man bustled off, and Bryant spent his time alone examining the surrounding people. In any other restaurant, the patrons might be looking at their phones or toying with tablets. Not here.

The Cosmos Club was where the most brilliant and celebrated minds in "science, literature, the arts, a learned profession, or public service" gathered, according to the club's promotional materials. *Not that they need to promote since they have exponentially more applicants than they have membership openings.* As such, the use of devices was strictly prohibited in the dining room to encourage discourse.

For those who wished to combine work and pleasure, the upstairs salons were well outfitted to handle all their technological needs. In this space, with its abundant wood paneling, patterned metal ceiling, and long, lush wooden bar that ran across one of the short walls, only conversation and contemplation were permitted.

He'd never before used this particular place to meet a contact. His only previous attendance had been to build up the history of the identity he was using, and he'd spent much of that time downing drinks at the bar alone. Representative Susan Moore arrived, and he stood to greet her, then waited for her to sit before reclaiming his seat. Old World manners were the rule of the day in the club, as well.

Before they could begin talking, the sommelier appeared with a bottle and two glasses. He offered Bryant a taste, but he deferred to his guest. She swirled it, sniffed it, and took a sip. "Excellent."

"Very good." The sommelier poured, and when he walked away, the server replaced him. "What is your dining pleasure this evening?"

Menus were a roll of the dice at the Cosmos Club. They didn't offer a full kitchen on certain evenings. Instead, one had a choice of four meals. He answered, "Surf and turf for me, please."

His guest nodded. "The same for me." The fact that neither of them had specified otherwise meant their steaks would be cooked medium rare, which was, in his opinion, the only acceptable choice. When he left, Susan said, "Nice place. First time I've been inside."

He chuckled. "I thought that might be why you chose the meeting location you did."

She grinned. "Guilty as charged."

"Don't keep me in suspense."

She laughed. "Just know that if you get this information and decide to bolt, I'm going to eat *your* dinner, too, and probably dessert afterward. And maybe another full bottle of wine because this is amazing. On your tab, of course."

He chuckled. "If I don't leave, you can still have all that, minus eating my food."

She nodded. "The spider in the center of the web seems to be one General Ehrlich. Or *a* spider, at least. He's throwing his weight around at high levels.

"That in itself isn't particularly notable. Lots of people play that game, but that he's doing it more or less invisibly to those lower in the hierarchy is. He's working through cutouts, which isn't the sort of behavior one expects from someone in his position. They tend to seek notoriety."

Bryant frowned. "That's equal parts unexpected and alarming."

"Agreed. It's particularly uncomfortable to see a military figure, rather than a politician, exerting that kind of authority."

"Incredibly useful stuff. Thanks for the information. Anything else?"

She shook her head and paused before replying as their server deposited an artfully arranged deconstructed salad in front of each of them. It involved greens, fruit, nuts, and a small pile of cheese that in itself probably cost as much as an entire dinner in a normal restaurant. After he departed, she said, "No, that's all I have. I had to call in a lot of favors to get this far. He's doing a solid job of keeping himself unnoticed."

"Sorry about that."

She waved the comment away. "Nah. That's the job. No big deal. It only means I have to start being nice to people now to get more favors later. I *hate* being nice."

Bryant chuckled, and for the rest of the exquisite meal, they shared normal conversation. Still, he couldn't shake the feeling that as dangerous as things had been before they knew about the general's involvement, they were now far more so.

CHAPTER TWENTY-SEVEN

The team gathered virtually over comms. Everyone was in their assigned location, and Diana, Rath, and Max had taken up residence in a small house in Indiana booked through a rental service. They'd never been there before that day, so it wasn't somewhere Serrano would think to look. The meeting had started with a discussion of Cara's recon on the bus. Diana said, "So, naturally, when Cara described the scene, I loved the idea of getting our property back."

A soft snort came from her second-in-command. Diana paused to let her speak, but she didn't follow it up. "Anyway, this is the perfect opportunity to punch Serrano right in the mouth. Figuratively, of course. Unless fate does us a solid and he's there. In that unlikely circumstance, I call dibs."

Rath added, "Secondses." Laughter sounded.

"In all seriousness, this seems like a strong play at this particular moment. I might've made it a little harder by sending that message to Serrano, but so be it. He knows the deal now. If they resist, they deserve what they get."

Hank asked, "So, we're going for a full lethal loadout?"

"That's our fallback position, so yes, gear up for it. We'll use the new grenades the techs and Ruby have put together for us and our existing nonlethals first. I expect there to be a surplus of guards so it might get messy."

Tony's voice conveyed his frown. "How exactly are we going to break in? I'm sure it's quite well-defended, right?"

Cara laughed. "That's putting it mildly. Secure outer perimeter, defenses on and around the building, and probably guards inside, although we can't verify that because they have effective jamming going on."

Diana replied, "We have a basic strategy, and we'll improvise on the fly. That's what we do. So, get your acts together and be at Ruby's bunker by eleven o'clock Eastern.

"That will be our gathering point to portal everyone to the warehouse Hank and Tony are securing for us in Hampton Roads. Except for Bryant and Sloan, who are sitting this one out. We'll gear up there and go get our truck back."

Their road cases were open, displaying each member's gear like a rock band or something. The building offered abundant space, so the team spread out at a comfortable distance. Work lights provided the illumination, and camp chairs took the place of benches. Cara was on Diana's left, and Rath on her right, with Max, as usual, at his side. The troll said, "Maybe I could carry a grenade launcher."

Diana chuckled. "At some point, sure. The three-twenty can be used on its own, as well as with a rifle. I think that tonight in particular, we don't want to mess with your aerodynamics."

"Logical. Maybe next time."

"Absolutely. The new ammunition is going to make a difference."

Rath grinned. "I especially like the sonic one."

She nodded. "Me too, buddy."

Between them, the techs and technomancers had successfully replicated two of the Army's experimental designs and added one of their own. The team now had knockout gas grenades, ones that deployed a kind of sticky trap, and an acoustic grenade modeled after the arrows they'd designed for Ruby's sister, Morrigan. People would become dizzy and nauseous while in proximity to the weapon. The increase in munition size meant they'd keep enemies out of operation for far longer than the archer's arrow-mounted version could.

As she made the connections between the cables in her base layer and the shock gloves to power them with the battery on the back of her belt, Cara asked, "So, I'm sure you thought of this already, but how will we keep the thing hidden afterward?"

Diana chuckled. "I wondered when someone was going to ask me that. Kayleigh and Deacon came through again. They figured out the inner workings of the military transponder system from the drones and reverse-engineered that, too.

"We plan to hide the bus more or less in plain sight as an Army vehicle. Its electronic skin can change to camouflage patterns with ease, and we'll spoof the right signals. No one should know. Of course, that depends on our drones taking out any they send to follow, but hopefully, we can manage it."

"If they can't, the turret on the top likely can."

"True enough. I've probably forgotten all the cool things the bus is capable of."

Cara gave a soft snort. "The most important thing recapturing it will accomplish is to keep Hank from moping around and being bored. If he's not up to his elbows in a project, he's not a happy person."

Diana frowned. "I gave him a project."

The other woman rolled her eyes. "Real estate is *not* his passion."

She laughed. "Yeah, I hear that. Make sure Hank gets the bag with the Army uniform in it. He'll have to change once we break away from the facility."

"Anything in particular you need me to do during the op?"

Diana shrugged. "Be exemplary, as always. Don't get killed. Keep an eye on Max."

Rath piped up from her side, "Where will Max be?"

She turned to him. "Deacon will put a couple of network enhancers on his harness. His job is going to be to sneak in with us, then find a hiding spot near the bus so Deacon can use the enhancers."

"Clever." The troll sounded impressed.

She grinned. "Thanks. I thought so. It's a task he's uniquely suited for, like you are for yours."

"You'll make sure Max is okay while I'm gone?"

Diana nodded. "You know we will." Her partner had

been more worried than usual about the dog since the arti-fact had made a move toward him. *Rightfully so. Scared us all.* "He'll be fine. I promise. Well, at least as fine as the rest of the team, anyway."

By two a.m., the planned launch time for the op, everyone was in position. Kayleigh and Deacon participated from Vegas, thanks to their apartment's powerful connection that presented virtually no lag in controlling their drones. The three advanced models they'd taken from the convoy were currently hovering above building tops a couple of blocks away from the facility holding the bus.

The drones had come with machine guns and missiles, the military friend or foe transponders, and a stealth skin with curves and angles designed to throw off sensors trying to detect them. They'd added two things, the caltrops module and the jamming suite.

In the process of modifying and testing them, the techs had learned enough about the drones to know their vulnerabilities, which gave them the confidence they'd be able to deal with the drone screen outside the facility. Reconnaissance had shown those were identical to the ones they now owned.

Kayleigh asked Deacon, "You ready?"

He nodded and cracked his knuckles. "As soon as Rath gets close enough, I'll be on the case."

"Don't screw it up."

"Thanks for the vote of confidence."

She chuckled. "Don't forget, confidence is sexy." She

turned back to face her displays and muttered, "All right, I guess it's time to get this show on the road." She activated her connection to the other agents. *Well, former agents, I suppose.* "Pregame check. Ground team ready?"

Each of the members of the ground team checked in. Kayleigh continued, "Troll Flight One ready?"

Rath's laugh came back across the calm. "Ready, ready, Roger, Roger."

She grinned. "Homebase is ready, too. What's the word, Boss?"

"Start the music."

CHAPTER TWENTY-EIGHT

Rath's goggles showed the techs' drones as they sped past his position in response to Diana's order to begin the op. He'd already configured his display, issuing Gwen a series of commands that would automatically take effect if and when circumstances changed. As the three drones flew toward the defensive drone screen, they would emit a jamming field that would essentially detach the enemy drones from their local supervision.

The techs said they'd probably hover in place when they lost signal but that they might also decide to start flying in random directions. From the first second of jamming, the people guarding the bus would be trying to regain control of them, so Rath had to go in immediately behind them, unable to wait and be sure they succeeded.

He leapt from the top of a factory smokestack a couple of blocks away and dropped precipitously to gain speed. Then he hit the button to open his wings, right on the mark Gwen had placed in his virtual path, and shifted upward, banking to the left.

His goggles showed potential paths in light yellow, and the route he should stay on in bright orange. That allowed him some indication of what might be coming next, but he couldn't be sure any of the lighter-colored winds would turn out to be viable. Ahead, the markings that represented the drones were jerking around, moving erratically within a small area.

So, they went a little haywire but not too crazy. Hope that doesn't mean the enemy is already regaining control of them.

If it did, it would blow their cover, and what they planned as a quick mission with limited risk would turn into something much more like an outright brawl. He banked to the left suddenly as the course changed, then dipped again, coming out of the dive in a serpentine to pass through more triangles.

He wasn't sure how Gwen was calculating his path but imagined it was a combination of air currents, sensor readings, and so forth. All he knew was that it was challenging, and because of that, fun.

Kayleigh said, "Okay, I'm pulling our drones back before the enemy catches on to what we're doing. Troll Flight One, you're on your own."

"Affirmative." Rath chewed his lip and focused on swerving appropriately to stay on the path Gwen had set for him. He made it over the top of the warehouse that held the bus and landed in a skid, his wings retracting the moment his feet were on the roof.

"Rerouting drones to the other side as a distraction. I'll let y'all know when they're ready," Kayleigh announced.

Rath removed the network enhancer box attached to his flight suit below his wings and placed it in the shelter of a large vent. He pushed the button to activate it, and the lights on the side blinked red, then glowed solid green.

A few seconds later, Deacon confirmed, "Enhancer active. I have a signal. Going in."

"Me too." Rath headed for the door that would take him down into the building so he could join the fight to come.

Diana led her team down the block, stopping on the opposite side of the street from the outermost counter-measures they'd identified earlier. They were all hidden under veils, hers covering Max and Cara shrouding Tony. Her display charted the sentries' walking paths, which changed when the drone interactions happened overhead.

A couple more people emerged from the building, and the existing guards shifted closer to the chain-link fence as if they expected something more might happen. She muttered, "Remember, hit fast, hit hard, get into the building."

Hank said, "We should go full-frontal assault on these people. We can totally take them."

Diana shook her head. "Settle down, Beavis. It'll be fine." He laughed like the cartoon character she'd called him, and a couple of chuckles came across the comm. "Glam, status?"

"Troll Flight successful. Deke found some unexpectedly robust countermeasures in place. He's swearing a lot and said something about *Pitfall*."

Diana frowned. "As in traps?"

"No. I don't think so. Pretty sure he's talking about the old video game on the Atari 2600 way back in the day."

Diana forced herself to relax. She didn't even remotely understand infomancy, so she had to trust Deacon knew what he was doing. A moment later, Kayleigh said, "Electronic defenses are down. Not sure for how long. Go."

Diana's initial plan had been to sneak past the outer cordon of guards and have Deacon lock down the building behind them. Like many initially great plans, it wouldn't work in practice. Even if they managed to fly over carrying Tony, the chances of them doing so silently enough to avoid notice were too high. So, she pivoted to something resembling the full-frontal assault Hank had recommended. As she ran forward, she said, "Diversion."

Kayleigh replied, "Affirmative." On the opposite side of the building, their drones would now swoop in and engage the ones in the defensive screen. Kayleigh had been sure she could strike with sufficient surprise to eliminate a couple of enemy craft with no significant damage to hers. The goal was to sow chaos, but keeping their military drones undamaged, preferably, and not destroyed, for certain, was a high priority.

Diana released the veil at the last possible moment and sent a blast of force magic into the large door in the chain-link fence. People and vehicles used the same entrance, so that particular piece of the outer defenses was about eight feet wide. It flew off its hinges and careened back to slam into the nearest sentries, who were still reacting with shock to the team's sudden appearance.

Her people ran through and launched force blasts and other magic at the nearby guards to prevent them from engaging. The goal was now to reach the building without getting bogged down outside. A drone flew at her from the left, and Diana sent a sizzling blast of lightning at it. When the two intersected, the aerial vehicle wobbled, then fell to slam to the ground inside the fence.

The next drone avoided her lightning, but a force shield prevented its machine gun rounds from reaching Diana. The drones they'd captured didn't have anti-magic bullet load-outs so the assumption was these wouldn't either. It was good to know they were correct. *We can't assume the same for the guards, unfortunately.*

They reached the heavy door that led into the facility, which had no obvious lock outside. Diana grabbed the handle and pulled, but it refused to open. The others gathered around her, raising shields and sending out magical attacks to keep the guards' heads down. "Deacon? Unlock the door. Please." She tried not to let her concern show in her voice.

He growled, "Yeah, go," and the lock *clicked*. She yanked the door open, waving her team through in front of her. Max was last in line, and she followed him in.

The interior was huge and looked more like an aircraft hangar than a warehouse. The outermost areas were empty, except for some supply boxes and other crates gathered in seemingly random spots. In the center of the wide expanse of concrete stood their mobile armory, a heavily modified eighteen-wheeler Hank had been instrumental in designing and acquiring.

Arranged in a rectangle around it was a mass of computer equipment, electronics, and even a couple of lasers visible from her current location. Also blocking them from their objective was a plethora of guards wearing black uniforms like the sentries outside, and holding rifles in guard position, something they'd likely been doing since the first moment their drones went haywire.

Diana announced, "Rabbit season. Stay safe." It was the signal for her team to separate and to use nonlethal force where possible. She ran off to the left, toward the nearest bundle of enemies, her task to reduce the enemy's numbers. Hank, Tony, Cara, and Max dashed in the opposite direction.

The plan was for Hank to focus on breaching the bus while taking care of any opposition that tried to stop him from reaching it. Tony was to find a useful position to put his grenade launcher, rifle, and huge pistol to work. Cara would provide overall defense after she escorted Max to his spot under the bus.

Adrenaline surged through Diana, and she grinned. *All right, Serrano. Let's see what you've got.*

CHAPTER TWENTY-NINE

Hank increased his lead over the others as they raced forward, single-minded in his determination to liberate the mobile armory from Serrano's people. He launched the gas grenade already loaded into his M203, rammed in the next experimental type, a sticky bomb, and fired it at a pair of enemies who'd turned their attention toward him and his allies.

The first caused those defenders to pull on masks, at least delaying them. The second was almost comical in how it latched onto the guards' boots and toppled them when they tried to take their next step.

He chuckled. "I knew hitting that convoy would turn out to be worthwhile, if only for the entertainment value." He loaded and dispatched a sonic grenade in the center of both pairs he'd engaged, and they suddenly found staying on their feet or getting back to their feet impossible. *Nice.*

More enemies emerged from around the front of the bus as he neared it. He dropped the rifle to hang on its strap and put on a burst of speed, reaching them before they could aim and fire.

A swipe of his hand knocked the rifles' barrels together, taking them both out of the picture for the moment, and landed a hard punch directly to the left enemy's face. His opponent looked stunned and staggered backward from the blow but didn't fall despite the additional electricity discharge from the shock glove.

Hank pulled back that fist, twisted his torso, and whipped it at his other foe's head. That one had time to react and managed to interpose the rifle along his attack path. He wound up punching the metal, which wasn't fun but didn't particularly hurt him.

He grabbed the weapon with that hand and landed a punch almost identical to the first with his right. The blast of electricity dropped the second guard. Hank hurled the gun across the warehouse, aiming for yet another pair of soldiers who were creeping around the side.

He missed, but their attempt to be secretive proved a double failure when a stun disc landed at their feet and took them both out of the battle. "Nice throw."

From behind him, Tony replied, "Thanks. Frisbee golf champion of my college."

Hank pointed at another group of soldiers. "How about you Frisbee or shoot them, too?"

"On it."

He trusted the gunslinger to take care of himself, so he slid under the truck. An array of electronics connected to the undercarriage, none of which belonged there. He pulled his multi-tool from his belt and extended the blade.

"All right. Time to figure out how you things connect and make it so you don't."

———

Cara slotted and launched grenades at every target she saw, both the new experimental kind and the older versions she'd included in her bandolier. A flash-bang took out a cluster, at least for the moment, and she followed it up with gas to catch them before their reeling senses allowed them to get their masks in place. In her ear, Deacon said, "Getting closer. Another ten feet or so."

She judged the distance and saw that position was ahead of the rearmost wheels of the mobile armory. She said, "Max," and when the dog looked at her, she pointed. "Under the truck, right in front of the back wheels, go."

The Borzoi took off, but before he could get there, a guard appeared from around the back of the bus and moved to intercept. Cara barked, "Max, defend," and the canine skidded to a stop, refocused on that guard, and leapt at him with a snarl.

The man tried to move his rifle, but Cara held it with telekinesis so he couldn't. She tore it away from him as the dog slammed into his chest, knocking him onto his back and causing his head to smack loudly on the floor. His helmet had likely protected him from serious damage, but he would see stars and hear bells.

"Max, under the truck." When the dog was clear, she threw a stun disc to take the guard out the rest of the way.

She realized the battle had split their forces, with Hank and Tony on the same side of the bus as she was and Diana alone on the other. She ran toward the trailer and gave herself a force boost at the last minute, doing a sort of half-fly half-jump up to its roof. Her landing required only a slight balance correction, which was an improvement from the norm. "Good news. Doesn't look like they've messed with the top at all."

Hank growled, "That's because they spent all their time sticking stuff on the bottom. Scumbags."

Cara lifted her launcher, loaded a sticky grenade, and fired it at a set of guards advancing on Diana. They froze in place, and she tossed another stun disc to knock them out. She turned in a circle and frowned. "Does it seem like there's a whole lot of bad guys here to anyone else?"

Diana answered, "Yeah, it does. They hoped we'd make a try for it." She side-kicked the guard nearest to her, sending them through the air to slam into the bus and crumple to the ground. She lifted a force-covered forearm to block the downward smash of the leftmost guard's rifle and used her right to create a wall of magic between her and another who was rushing in. He slammed into it, bounced off, and staggered backward a few steps.

Another of the four that surrounded her tried for his weapon again. As soon as his hands got near it, she yanked it downward with telekinesis, forcing him to bend over. She was conserving her strength, or she would've taken it away from him entirely.

She'd already used her energy capsule in an earlier situation where she was outnumbered and had no time to fish her flask out of her pouch. In the meantime, it was enough to make sure they couldn't bring their guns into the fight. Because, hand-to-hand, they didn't have a chance.

She heard gunshots but knew it was unlikely they'd aimed at her. She was right in the center of the clustered guards, and it would be foolish for any of the ones farther away to take shots at her for fear of hitting their people.

Sometimes what you wanted turned out to be what you needed. She *needed* the safety of several enemies around her to avoid getting shot from a distance. She *wanted* to lay into them with fists and feet, let them outnumber her, then realize the dramatic miscalculation they'd made. With every blow, she imagined she was sending a message to Kevin Serrano and his people.

Diana kicked another one out of the way, and her shock gloves bashed a third into oblivion. Then gunfire came at her, forcing her to drop and roll. She slipped through a gap in the equipment that surrounded the bus and rose to a crouch behind it. The shooter was visible from that angle, standing near the warehouse's outer skin, their rifle poised to fire if she showed any part of her body.

She also saw the troll gliding down toward that person and watched in satisfaction as Rath collapsed his wings and landed hard on the guard, slamming them back into the wall and down to the floor. He pulled out his baton and tapped them with the shock tip to finish the fight. She dashed over and offered him a medium five, which for him was a high five. "Nice work, buddy."

He nodded. "You too. Max is safe?"

"I saw him under the bus. He has a solid defensive position. No one will mess with him."

"Good."

They turned as a nearby sound suggested more guards had gotten their act together and were coming toward them. Diana said, "Time to take out the trash."

The situation changed dramatically for the worse as a portal suddenly opened ten feet away, and men and women in military fatigues stepped through it. A moment later, she and Rath faced five fully equipped soldiers, some of whom, instead of raising their rifles, lifted riot shields with one arm and cast spells with the other.

CHAPTER THIRTY

Diana snapped, "Army's here. Duck season. Keep safe." The command would instruct her team to switch to lethal force as needed. Behind the soldiers, Serrano's people faded into the background, apparently leaving the battlefield. She didn't quite understand why they'd do that unless they were as surprised by the Army's appearance as she was. *Doesn't matter. Focus, Diana.*

She summoned a shield to protect her from the incoming spells and fired her rifle at the nearest enemy's head. He crouched behind his riot shield and the anti-magic bullets careened off it. Two of the five dispatched rounds in return while the others cast spells again. Rath scampered off to the left, and Diana launched herself into the air to avoid the barrage.

Tony said, "Just to confirm, duck season."

"Confirmed. Five on my side." Diana sounded harried.

"Five here, as well. Hercules?"

"Busy. It's all you, bro."

Tony gave a small laugh and shifted slightly to keep the equipment he'd crouched behind between him and the soldiers. "Croft?"

She responded immediately, "What do you need?"

"Distract them for a minute if you'd be so kind."

"Right."

The comment turned out to be an acknowledgment and an indication of her direction as she ran on a diagonal away from the truck, throwing bursts of magic at the five soldiers. They promptly faced her, three of them countering with spells and two firing weapons.

Tony hoped she'd be safe, but his focus was solely on his targets. He rose from his cover position, ignoring the cramp in his side that tried to distract him and limit his motion. He raised his rifle and aimed carefully, then smoothly pulled the trigger.

Three rounds punched into the first soldier, followed by three into the second, taking down both of those firing at Cara. He'd struck them each in the upper thigh, a spot he'd chosen deliberately. It would give them a chance of survival, but only if they evacuated immediately.

He traversed his aim to the remaining enemies, but they'd reacted to the unexpected barrage defensively, crouching behind their riot shields and throwing up barriers of magic around them. They did the right thing, opening a portal and dedicating two of their number to take the wounded away while the last stood guard.

Tony nodded, respecting the decision, and kept his weapon trained on the fifth in case he should falter with the angle of his shield. If Cara were up, she would surely smack him down in short order while he split his attention. He reported, "Two down, two busy."

A fireball smacked into the front of the bus, causing Hank to cringe reflexively. He shouted, "Cut it out, you people," and continued in a calmer tone, "Deke, where are we?"

The infomancer replied, "Bus systems are active. I have a signal, thanks to Max. I'll log in and open it up."

Hank grinned and pulled another piece of equipment away from the trailer's underside. He shook his head and muttered, "Morons."

A moment later, Deacon said in a voice full of concern, "Wait a minute. Gotta check something."

Hank frowned and kept ripping things off the undercarriage until he'd gotten them all. He spotted legs to his right, moving slowly forward. The camouflage trousers told him it wasn't a friendly so he rolled silently out from under the vehicle and rose into a crouch behind them. The soldier didn't notice. His attention focused on Diana and Rath, who were both being evasive near the edge of the warehouse.

Hank stomped forward, grabbed the man by the collar, and pulled backward, hurling him against the side of the trailer. He danced in and delivered six punches in quick succession, two to the man's legs, two to his sides under his vest's protection, and two to his head, the first knocking it to the right and the second blasting the soldier into unconsciousness. Satisfied, he reported, "One more down."

Deacon said, "Damn bastard infomancers. They're waiting for me to log in. They'll try to use my signal as a channel to hack into the bus since they couldn't break in themselves."

"So that's why it's still here. Double trap."

"Yep. Scumbags."

Hank reached down and grabbed the enemy's fallen shield, sliding it onto his left arm. "So, get in there and fix it."

He heard Deacon's scowl. "Working on it."

The conversations held by his teammates had been playing in Rath's ear while he did his best to scamper away from the people attempting to shoot him or throw magic at him. They'd kept him on the run, so he hadn't had a chance to counterattack or properly break off pursuit. *Annoyingly competent. Of course, there are five of them and only one of me.*

Deacon said, "Rambo, need you to do something."

He launched into a dive and roll to avoid the fireball that tried to cook him. "Okay."

"Switch to electrical." Rath complied, and one lens of his goggles displayed the power running through the place. He made sure to spin in a complete circle so the infomancer would get the view he wanted. Then he cut sharply, changing direction to avoid rushing into the gunsight of the man who was pointing a rifle ahead of his path.

Deacon growled, "There's nothing there." Then a note of suspicion entered his tone. "They couldn't be that stupid, could they? Is there an office or an area that's kind of separated from the rest of the place?"

Rath replied, "Stand by," grabbed two smoke grenades from his belt, and slammed them down at his feet. When they'd obscured his position, he fired his grapnel up and let the motor carry him up toward the ceiling. He laughed inwardly, channeling his best Michael Keaton. *I'm Batman. Wait. I'm BatTroll.* When he reached the gridwork that ran under the roof, he crouched to avoid being seen from below and surveyed the area. He found what Deacon had mentioned on the front side of the building, opposite from where they'd come in. "Yep. Got one."

"Heat mode."

Rath complied, and the whole warehouse shifted into an array of moving blobs of color. "Looks like two people sitting back-to-back."

Deacon replied, "They're clever bastards. Go teach them what we do to clever bastards."

He laughed. "Happy to." He leapt from crossbeam to crossbeam, making his way above the battle, hoping no one would notice him. When he arrived at the far end, he used the grapnel again, this time to lower him quietly onto the roof of the small structure.

He dropped from there to the floor and opened the door as silently as he could. As expected, two people sat in the room facing opposite directions with their attention entirely focused on the computer rigs in front of them.

Rath drew his batons and crept forward, then flicked them out to full extension and stabbed them into both figures' shoulders. The man on his left and the woman on his right twitched and shuddered, then slumped uncon-scious in their chairs. He laughed. "Easy as pie."

A moment later, with what sounded like great satisfac-tion, Deacon said, "Hercules, your chariot awaits."

Cara leapt down from the top of the bus as she saw four soldiers closing on Diana. She landed next to the boss, who turned to face the threat. Diana smiled. "Good to see you."

Cara laughed. "I know you could've handled them on your own, but I thought I'd join."

"I think it's time we show these chuckleheads a lesson."

"Agreed. What are you thinking?"

Diana pulled her sword, and Cara responded by drawing Angel and Demon. "So, old-school. Works for me."

The boss nodded. "First, let's take away their toys."

Cara and Diana reached out with their telekinesis and ripped the shields off their foes' arms, throwing them away before they could react to save them. Next, they tore the enemies' weapons from their grasps, hurling them away as well, until it was magic versus magic and swords, aside from the pistols at their hips.

Diana charged forward, and Cara did the same a moment behind her. The boss angled toward the pair on her side, so Cara curved a little to the left, trying to force the four to separate a little. One of them pulled their pistol, so she changed the angle of her run, now heading straight for them, and reached out with her telekinesis to grab a fallen shield. After using it to deflect the bullets, she hurled it at the soldier, who used his magic to knock it out of the way.

A fireball reached her, one she'd seen coming and could have actively defended against but had decided to let her deflector handle. It sucked in the magic, and she grinned at the shocked expression on the soldier's face. She shouted, "Aww, didn't your spell work, scumbag?"

The enemy in front of her called up a pair of magical shields and used them to deflect Cara's first two dagger attacks. He tried for a front kick, and Cara skipped away in the direction of his partner, turning the evasion into a full-on sidekick. The second soldier brought a hand down to knock her foot to the floor before it could reach him, but that left him in a slightly awkward position with his shoulder lowered.

She pulled Angel across her body as a wind-up and stabbed it deep into the back of that shoulder, causing the soldier to cry out in pain and go down on one knee. She wrenched the blade free with a twist, then turned back to the first person, who looked appropriately worried at the loss of their ally.

Cara tried a front kick, but her foe brought the shields forward to block it. She pointed Angel and cast lightning through it, encompassing her enemy. The soldier was smart enough to summon a full body shield in the instant before it hit, so while it might've caused them some pain, it didn't take them out of the fight.

Cara's next move did, however. She dashed forward and spun into a leg sweep, which her enemy reflexively tried and failed to jump. *Should've trusted your shield.* The man landed awkwardly on the floor, and Cara kicked him in the head, holding back a large portion of the potential force of the blow. At the moment they were stunned from the fall and the kick, she delivered them to full unconsciousness with a tap from her stun glove.

She crossed to the other soldier, who'd managed to get to his feet with his arm dangling strangely and overwhelmed him with punches until she connected with one to the face that took him out as well. She saw that Diana had defeated hers and turned to look for more enemies. At that moment, Hank announced, "Everyone on board. We're out of here."

Cara ran to the side door, which had popped open, and jumped into the trailer, followed shortly by Diana. Tony and Max entered from the rear, and the truck started to roll. Diana asked, "What about Rambo?"

Rath replied, "Riding shotgun."

Everyone laughed at that. The interior of the mobile armory had several strategically placed monitors. All of them were live, showing feeds from the cameras mounted around the truck. Hank rammed it through the garage door, which offered minimal resistance.

Once they were outside, the turret on top extended and started firing, sending soldiers who might've thought about pursuing diving for cover. Hank put his foot down, and the truck surged forward. They'd all memorized the route out of the facility and onto the nearest highway, which was where they planned to lose their pursuit.

Hank said, "Drones. Ralph, assign offensive turret to Agent Benoit. Maintain automatic control of defensive turret."

Cara chuckled, having forgotten the truck's AI was

named Ralph for the movie character that liked to break things. She sat on a bench as her display became the roof turret's sights. It was in automatic mode, so all she had to do was designate targets and determine priorities. She did so through a combination of eye-tracking and blinking, a particular set of patterns she hadn't used in a long, long time. The guns fired steadily, the cannon taking out every drone it detected and she selected.

Deacon said, "That's the last of them. Once you're on the highway, change the skin whenever you're out of overhead view, and do what you can to play a shell game with the other semis. By the time they get satellite footage online, I'll have planted enough diversions that they won't be able to find you. Nice job, everyone."

A spontaneous cheer went up, and Diana asked, "Rambo, is Hercules crying?"

The troll giggled in response. "Yes. Yes, he is."

CHAPTER THIRTY-ONE

His building's conference room was decidedly not large enough to hold all the egos currently inside it. Kevin and Tash held down one side of the long rectangular table.

Directly opposite him was Senator Richardson, with Senator Borowski to his left, Kevin's right. Their assistants sat on the left-hand side of the table from his perspective, as did Kiki Shelford from the FBI and Andrea Walsh from Homeland Security. *Their* assistants sat across the table from them, as did a man in an Army dress uniform with a nameplate reading Shalls.

Richardson asked, "How the hell did you screw this up so badly, Serrano?"

So that's how it's going to be. Kevin shrugged. "I'd like to remind the oversight committee that they approved this plan, just for the record. We're not up against amateurs, as they keep reminding us.

"The trap was a good one, several layers deep, and Sheen managed to defeat every last one of them. My infomancers are working on verifying if the worm they *think* they loaded into the truck's software is viable." He shrugged again. "Worst case, we find them again when they use the damn thing. It's not exactly subtle or easy to hide."

Borowski replied, "Easy enough to hide that it eluded your efforts to catch it."

Tash bristled at his side, and he tapped her leg under the table to remind her to keep it calm. They'd both known this sort of grilling would come after any unsuccessful op because the committee would feel the need to flex their authority, and this was a notable failure.

Borowski said, "It *is* a point in your favor that even the Army wasn't able to turn the tables."

Serrano kept his face neutral. No one had read him into the part of the plan where the Army responded, and that irked him far more than a little. When Colonel Nance had explained the hierarchy to him, he hadn't been exaggerating. Kevin had thought he was near the top of the pile, but as it turned out, his position was more like the middle. *And falling, probably.*

He faced the Army officer. "I'm surprised not to see Colonel Nance here today."

The man gave a short nod. "He's unavailable."

Shelford asked, "And Major Leland?"

"Also unavailable." The oversight committee spent the next interminable length of time questioning the lieutenant, and he answered, deflected, and generally seemed unconcerned that his area of the operation was being blamed for failure as well. When he looked down at his watch for the third time in as many minutes, it rubbed Kevin's instincts the wrong way.

He gave a hand signal to Tash to make sure she was aware of it. She returned one that indicated she was. *What the hell are you up to, Lieutenant Shalls?*

The questioning continued, eventually coming back to him, and the senators got into what Kevin thought of as their campaigning mode. They made grandiose statements in dramatic voices and did everything short of pounding on the table to make sure he felt every inch of his failure. He was about to calmly reply to another of their endless, infuriating questions when an alarm shrieked in his earpiece.

Several things happened in the moment that followed. First, Tash slammed into him, the initial part of a move that would carry him to the floor. Second, a portal appeared behind the Army officer's chair, and he pushed off the table, toppling backward through the magical opening.

Third, and perhaps most importantly, he was granted the chance to see the incredibly shocked looks on the faces of the oversight committee as the room, and presumably the building, collapsed or exploded around them with a roar.

THE STORY CONTINUES

A new side has declared itself in the battle for control of the Rhazdon artifacts spreading evil through the country. It's up to Diana, Rath, Cara, and their team to stay focused on what really matters: keeping artifacts out of the hands of those who would misuse them. Continue the fight in *ROGUE AGENTS ON THE HUNT*.

AUTHOR NOTES - TR CAMERON

NOVEMBER 9, 2021

Four books in! Thank you for reading the further adventures of Sheen and company, and for taking a look at the author notes, too.

I didn't plan for the last chapter. I mean, I knew that Kevin and Tash had to face the oversight committee, but I thought it would be a *figurative* explosion, you know? But sometimes things just spill out onto the page, and you can't take them back. (Yes, of course you *can*, but probably shouldn't)

I'm missing the 20Books conference in Vegas right now, and it's a bummer. That conference, in addition to the monthly get-togethers Martha hosts, recharges my author battery. I've been to all the conferences except this one. But covid would be extra bad for people in my household due to other medical issues, so have to play it entirely safe.

So, I'm home. Working, writing, planning the next series to pitch it to Martha and Michael. Taking the kid out to a hotel at the beach for a few days soon, which will be cold as heck, but it gets them out of the house.

I lost interest in *Mass Effect*. I might get back to it. That means my last two game purchases (remember *Humankind*, which I still don't understand?) were busts. I'm leery of purchasing any others at this point. I hear the new *Guardians of the Galaxy* is worth playing. Maybe I'll wait for a sale.

What I *am* playing, and *way* too much, is *Fortnite*. I get why it's popular. And the monetization is brilliant. All cosmetic and entertaining. They've got some clever storytellers and brilliant artists on their team. The whole house has the bug – the kid is the best at it, my wife (who prefers to solo) is second best, and I generally play the sacrificial target that reveals where the enemy is when they kill me so my team can take them down.

To be fair, that's more or less been my role in team games since *World of Warcraft*. Healer and sacrificial offering.

I followed Will Wheaton from Ready Player Two on audio to John Scalzi's *The Last Emperox*. I loved it when I read it, and if anything, I love it more in audio. Classic sci-fi goodness.

Speaking of amazing sci-fi. *Dune*. Seriously. I loved it. LOVED it. Gorgeous. Maybe a little slow, but that's in keeping with the tone of the story. Every performance was great, although I don't think I can handle Jason Momoa without a beard. I'm very happy the sequel telling the second half of the story has gotten the green light for production to begin.

Soon I will pit myself against the task of replacing a hinge on my wife's laptop. Judging by prior experience, it's going to go *really* well (Yes, that's sarcasm). After that, trying to install a wireless camera in the little house my wife and kid have put on the porch to house their adopted chipmunk. Again, will likely go *flawlessly*. (His name is Chonk. He's adorable.)

Reminder again - If you're not part of the Oriceran Fans Facebook group, join! There's a pizza giveaway every month, and Martha and (usually) I and all sort of fun author folks show up via Zoom to chat with our readers. It's a great time, and the community feel to it is truly fantastic. Oriceran Fans. Facebook. Your phone is probably within reach. Do it!

Before I go, once again, if this series is your first taste of my Urban Fantasy, look for "Magic Ops." I promise you'll enjoy it, and you'll get more of Diana, Rath, and company. You might also enjoy my science fiction work. All my writing is filled with action, snark, and villains who think they're heroes. Drop by www.trcameron.com and take a look!

Until next time, Joys upon joys to you and yours – so may it be.

PS: If you'd like to chat with me, here's the place. I check in daily or more: https://www.facebook.com/ AuthorTRCameron. Often I put up interesting and/or silly content there, as well. For more info on my books, and to join my reader's group, please visit www.trcameron.com.

AUTHOR NOTES - MARTHA CARR

DECEMBER 7, 2021

It's the end of the year, at last. Time for a little gratitude, especially this year.

For some this may have felt like the year whizzed by but mine was a little strange. It started in January with a broken arm, which was kind of big news for me. Normally, things float along for me, and all is well. It happened while walking Leela when I tripped in a gopher hole. Go figure. Leela was busy sniffing something wonderful and didn't even notice I had gone splat on the pavement.

Whatever. The year moved on and I finally got around to seeing a doctor for the first time post-Covid and things popped up like I was playing whack-a-mole. Let's shorten this part to say there were a lot of the routine tests you don't want to do, but you have to do – and then a few surprises that ended up in surgery three times in six weeks.

I was drunk on anesthesia for most of the spring.

Then cancer returned – third stage melanoma and by now I was kind of tired of being poked and prodded and wanted to go hang out in my garden instead. I probably said that a few times. Fortunately, people listened and nodded and pointed out that this too would have to be dealt with. One more surgery and then chemo.

Woof, chemo. Just hearing the word gets me to slowly shake my head.

I ended up driving to MD Anderson, the epicenter for melanoma, once a month where I found such great doctors, nurses, technicians. Fans got together amongst themselves and secretly plotted to send me direct messages with long stories to entertain me. Flowers arrived from Denmark, hot chocolate from someone in the states, and a small Buddha from upstate New York, and chocolates. A neighbor knit a shawl to keep me warm sitting in the recliner during infusions.

Meanwhile, the world slowed down for me and my energy drained quickly in the afternoons.

But I was determined to not let this year be about chemo or surgery or anything medical. Instead, I looked for the gifts that I knew had to be there. Frankly, are always there but normally I'm too busy to look. Always another book to write.

The gifts were the people right around me who had my back. Charley, who writes the Finnegan Dragonbender series, and showed up on loan from his wife to fix things around the house and do all the cooking for a week. Michael who kept calling just to chat and make jokes. Analise who kept me entertained with the most fabulous stories. She's been on the Moth Stage a few times and is amazing. Or Meg who sent a coloring book that was called, Fuck Cancer. It was funny.

But there were also too many people I thought of as

'friends' who I only got a quick text from once in a while, if that.

That's not a complaint, merely an observation that told me I was calling too many people a friend, when acquaintance was more accurate. That led to the next question – was I tending to too many people and not enough on the core, small group that are really friends. Some reorganizing ensued. Kind of like mindful friendships.

Another was it really sunk in that if I don't really get healthy with food and exercise, it's going to have an outsized negative impact on my quality of life today. Not tomorrow or sometime in the future. Right now. But, if I was going to do something for longer than a summer or at best, a year or two it had to be choices I like.

So, I found yoga and swimming and boxing and riding a bike. Mindful exercise. And I got better, easy to use cookbooks and figured out how to cook fish, which I love but didn't think I could do it justice at home. Not true. Just took a little practice, some directions and patience. The usual approach. Mindful eating.

I took a look at my work life and in that area, I love exactly where I am and where I'm heading, and I'm still open to whatever pops up along the way. That one is kind of rolling along, which is always nice to be able to say.

Back to this being the end of the year – and thankfully, the end of chemo. I can take all of this new realignment with me into 2022 and see where it leads. A gentle kind of refresh. More adventures to follow.

OTHER SERIES IN THE ORICERAN UNIVERSE:

THE LEIRA CHRONICLES
CASE FILES OF AN URBAN WITCH
SOUL STONE MAGE
THE KACY CHRONICLES
MIDWEST MAGIC CHRONICLES
THE FAIRHAVEN CHRONICLES
I FEAR NO EVIL
THE DANIEL CODEX SERIES
SCHOOL OF NECESSARY MAGIC
SCHOOL OF NECESSARY MAGIC: RAINE CAMPBELL
ALISON BROWNSTONE
FEDERAL AGENTS OF MAGIC
SCIONS OF MAGIC
THE UNBELIEVABLE MR. BROWNSTONE
DWARF BOUNTY HUNTER
ACADEMY OF NECESSARY MAGIC
MAGIC CITY CHRONICLES

OTHER BOOKS BY JUDITH BERENS

OTHER BOOKS BY MARTHA CARR

JOIN THE ORICERAN UNIVERSE FAN GROUP ON FACEBOOK!

CONNECT WITH THE AUTHORS

TR Cameron Social

Website: www.trcameron.com

Facebook: https://www.
facebook.com/AuthorTRCameron

Martha Carr Social

Website: http://www.marthacarr.com

Facebook: https://www.facebook.com/
groups/MarthaCarrFans/

Michael Anderle Social

Website: http://lmbpn.com

Email List: http://lmbpn.com/email/

https://www.facebook.com/LMBPNPublishing

https://twitter.com/MichaelAnderle

https://www.instagram.com/lmbpn_publishing/

https://www.bookbub.com/authors/michael-anderle

BOOKS BY MICHAEL ANDERLE

Sign up for the LMBPN email list to be notified of new releases and special deals!

https://lmbpn.com/email/

For a complete list of books by Michael Anderle, please visit:

www.lmbpn.com/ma-books/

Made in the USA
Las Vegas, NV
11 October 2023